Preface

Sarah Sandlin is a modern, red-haired, blue-eyed American widow obsessed with her love of genealogy. She works from home, where her self-imposed solitude receives few interruptions.

When a letter from Thomas Smith arrives and invites her to the U.K. to research his family's history, she ventures out of her comfort zone and travels to his Yorkshire estate, Highbridge. A fascinating trail of clues opens up, sending them on a road trip to Aberdeen Scotland to discover answers. Can she be content with her quiet life again?

This is a modern romance and a genealogical mystery mixed with an inside look at life on a large country estate. Sarah becomes invested in the family and as Christmas approaches, she must choose to close a long open door or return home to the U.S.A.

Look For Other Books By Linda J Pifer

Ohio Girl

A memoir of childhood and three generations.

Illus. 92 pictures, 122 pages

(At https://www.lindajpiferauthor.com only)

Daniel Smith-New Zealand Passage

Book Two in the Windows Trilogy –

Fiction – 385 pages

From Scotland and its Depression in 1847 to the south island of New Zealand, Daniel searches for a new beginning in the island's young settlement.

Copper Swift-Back to Highbridge

Book Three in the Windows Trilogy

Fiction – 302 pages

Two generations face losing Highbridge, their ancestral estate in North Yorkshire and a mysterious stranger walks at night in the halls. The Estate's fate rests on their success.

Visit the author's website at:

https://www.lindajpiferauthor.com

Linda J Pifer

WINDOWS

Book One

Cover design by Linda J Pifer
Cover photo Woman at Window;
Gannavasylenko|Dreamstime.com
Cover photo Florida Sunrise by Author

Published by Readingseat Books

ISBN 13-978-9890142-2-9

Printed by Createspace, an Amazon.com company

Revised July 2016

To John Roger

who provides just the right amount of
love, humor and distraction.

Thanks and Appreciation

To my family for giving me room to create.

Thanks Also To:

Terry Gilbert Fellows at Blackheath Dawn Writers
Limited©
for putting up with this Yankee and correcting
my words to his side of the pond.

Jacqueline Piepenhagen
Poetess, Novelist, First Reader.

Anne Cunningham, Beta Reader Extraordinaire.

Chapter 1 London Invitation

The letter comes by special delivery, postmarked 'London'. The mailman, whose knock interrupted my morning's work, retreats to his rolling mailbag. I shut the door and toss the envelope to my desk where it joins the rest of the paper stored there in various heaps.

The following day it lays partially buried among the morning's research notes; I recognise it beside my clock which tells me I've missed lunch – again.

"Okay, let's see what this is all about," I mutter and open the envelope on the way to the kitchen. Talking to myself seems to be happening more often I note.

August 19, 2010

Dear Ms. Sandlin,

I am a descendent of Charles Regis Smith through his son Stephen R. Smith and noticed your recent queries on the genealogy network for a Smith connection in Europe. I feel quite possibly your research into Brian Smith's line might give you a corner on our line as well; who knows, we might be cousins.

I invite you to accept my offer for employment and conduct our family's genealogy research. The subject is new to me and more time-consuming than I

1

*am able to dedicate to at this time. However, I do
realise its importance to my family.*

*You will want to verify my credentials, of course,
and please contact my ex-wife, Lydia Williams, at
(LWill@Highb.co.uk) in regard to my character.*

*If you find an interest in this project, please reply
via my cell number listed below to discuss further.*

Sincerely,

Thomas Vail Smith

Interesting and a little flattering that someone would
consider me but, I'm not interested. The letter and its
vellum envelope are deposited in the trash can and I vow
not to think about it again.

After a long sip of iced tea, I turn to stare out the
kitchen window into the backyard. The pool water slowly
stirs the leaves blown from the live oak tree during last
night's storm. I need to get out there and clean up, but
when I open the patio door, hot humidity fogs the cold
glass in my hand.

Okay, this is all the fresh air I need and withdraw to
reconsider my good intentions for the yard. Just before
the door slides to a close, my resident yellow tiger cat
Tom dodges from under a porch chair to make a run for
it, barely getting through before it shuts.

"Tom. You lucky son of a feline, your tail was almost
shortened." But I realise I can't really be mad at my one

true companion who inspires my smile with his fur sticking up from the humidity.

"Bad hair day too buddy?" He gazes unblinking at me as I look into his eyes. You're as easy to be around as Brian my old friend, lucky for me you showed up. I've always wondered if you might be his spirit, but I know that's ridiculous though.

For some reason, while finishing off some leftover pizza, I again reach to retrieve the letter for one more read.

Whatever this guy is up to, I think it's risky to answer him; he probably paid someone to vouch for his character. *Who would refer to his ex for anything?* I roll my eyes and toss the letter back into the trash then head to bathroom for a shower.

Wrapped in a towel, I look into my two blue eyes staring back from the mirror. I used to be up for an adventure if it took me out of the box, but lately my life is on a rut into the future. I won't let my curiosity pull me back to the letter; he couldn't possibly be related...could he?

Brian's death left a big hole in you I acknowledge directly to the mirror's reflection. Feeling the familiar grief descend, I hang my head as it washes over me again; his annual checkup, cancer in his right lung and surgery. My dear husband Brian, dead within four months, the first two years of utter helplessness and grief sucking me down despite my parents' efforts to comfort me.

The first time I talked openly about it to anyone, including my parents, was to Judy my closest friend from high school. It was a quiet winter evening and she listened silently without trying to offer meaningless niceties, allowing me to cry when it became too much. The bottle of wine slowly went empty between us, poured out with the grief I'd bottled up inside. We sat for a while staring into the crackling fire in a rush of quiet then she stood up to look at the pictures of Brian on the mantle and asked 'What now?'

"What do you mean?" I responded.

"I need someone to write manager training manuals for me and you could do it," She said.

"Why would you want me for that job?"

"I think you need a diversion." She smiled at me.

I remember hesitating then I glanced down at my rumpled pj's worn all day and realised my hair probably matched.

"Do you think?" I said and we both started to laugh. It felt so good to laugh after years without it.

That was seven years ago; do I need another diversion, I wonder?

I'm calling it a night and walk through the house to turn out the lights, but hesitate at the wastebasket to pull out Mr. Thomas Vail Smith's crumpled letter one last time.

Guess it wouldn't hurt to give him a call; I feel the old tightness begin to build in the pit of my stomach. I stare at the envelope; it represents everything I've managed to hide from all these years. Despite my fear, I put the envelope on top of the hallway chest as a reminder for the next morning and feel slightly better.

Early morning sun shines under the shutters and Tom sits nearby, his green eyes balefully fixed on me.

"Okay mister give me a minute and we'll see about breakfast. I know you want to play, but it's not in the cards this morning. Go on, I've got to straighten up the bed."

I give him a playful push toward the edge, "Shoo!"

He jumps to a graceful landing then strolls in the direction of the kitchen. Glancing at the clock, breakfast might be in order before launching a call to the U.K.. I detour first to the front porch and collect the morning newspaper. Whew, the humidity is already climbing and it's still early.

Tom predictably waits in the kitchen and rubs across my legs to coax for attention, but most of all, his food.

"Okay, okay – you're first on the list" After opening a can of gourmet food and changing his drinking water, it's finally my turn. The fridge yields eggs and a fresh orange; give me coffee and I'm set.

As usual, a cursory glance at the newspaper produces a frown; murders and thefts described in more detail than I need to know are the reasons I rarely read beyond the headlines. The one sane thing to do is go directly to the comics where my favorite characters keep me grounded. I'll catch up later on the internet - maybe.

Breakfast and dishes done, I'm out of excuses and decide to make the call from the kitchen table.

'Hello, this is Thomas Smith' runs the recording. Startled at its suddenness, I realise the recorder has dead air.

"Hi, this is Sarah Sandlin" I blurt out. "I received your letter yesterday and wanted to speak with you in person. I find your letter intriguing but would like to discuss the offer with you before making a decision. You can reach me at my home number 352-570-1245. Thank you."

I take my cell phone with me to the den and sit down to my laptop. No use taking his 'ex-wife's' word for it; let's just see what you've been up to Mr. Smith.

I enter his name on a search and am surprised to see an article come up immediately from the London edition of the Financial Times. 'A well-known import firm Smith Imports Limited of London announced this week that Stephen Smith, CEO and Chairman of the Board, along with his son Thomas Smith, Director of Marketing, will leave the organization in pursuit of other interests. Stephen Smith, whose father founded the Company, will remain on the board of directors as a member and consultant.'

No pictures in the article but I do have my imagination. Oh yeah, he's middle aged, a typically stodgy businessman and I'm thinking eyes: imperceptibly cold and gray.

Another article comes up and this one has a picture. Okay, I am so wrong.

I gaze at a very nice pair of brown eyes on a well turned out and seemingly fit gentleman in his late 30's. He's building a mill somewhere in Yorkshire; what a switch in direction, from the import business to millwork.

"Why does he look familiar?" I reach for the magnifying glass from the desk drawer but try as I might, I can't place him. Well, I haven't been to the U.K. for years and I certainly haven't met any Brits in Florida. At least my earlier imagined 'slasher' and 'scammer' profiles can be eliminated, unless they fall under his 'other interests', which I doubt.

I forward the web page to an old school friend and ask him to check Mr. Smith's background as a favor. I consider calling the ex-wife as suggested but I'll put that bit of joy off for a while and return to research into the birth records on Brian's grandfather.

Later I reluctantly admit to reaching a 'brick wall'; out of the plethora of Smiths in the European community, none seem to fit his family. I hate reaching this point but no use procrastinating; a chart of the previous families I've reviewed may uncover something missed on their timelines. It's a process of elimination and I'll include multiple spellings just in case his family's name evolved over the ages; Smythe, Smit, and other hyphenated versions may turn up something new, too. Ah well, a needle in a haystack perhaps, but I have time to spare.

It's intriguing to look at new families different from those I've been working on. The drama in earlier times is fascinating and sometimes heartwrenching; wars won and lost, sickness claiming children and adults, people struggling to settle new countries and fortunes won only to be lost again.

The intensity of it all makes me appreciate what I have today; two parents in a nearby town who love me, a good job, a roof over my head and medical care way beyond what prior generations could have imagined. It wasn't enough for Brian though was it; the oft repeated question comes again and I demand, when will there be a cure?

The phone's melody snatches me out of my concentration. I demand aloud "What now" then punch the speaker button and answer, "Hello."

A voice on the other end cautiously replies "Good evening...Sarah?" A male caller who's quietly Brit brings me back to reality and I realise who it must be.

"Yes, this is Sarah."

"This is Thomas Smith in London. I received your message this afternoon, but waited until I got back to my flat to call; not too late I hope?"

"No, not at all." The clock reads eleven pm. Another day without dinner and Tom sits on top of my desk glaring at me rather miffed that his bowl went empty hours ago.

"I've been busy myself and lost track of time. How are you?" At that point Tom begins his loudest meowing reserved for dire situations.

"Very well, thank-you and you?" he asks in that suave manner I love to hear.

"I'm well thank-you; just working on a personal genealogy project." I get up from the chair, switch from speaker to receiver and walk to the kitchen with Tom on my heels.

"I've been assisting my father in a business venture and have a new appreciation for working late hours, too." He says.

Oh yes," as I reach under the sink for a cat food can. "I read the article about you and your father and Smith Imports on the net." I instantly regret revealing I've been surfing the net for him and hope he doesn't catch on, but too late.

"Why yes," he replies in surprise, "I guess it's pretty widely known to anyone who's curious."

I hesitate with the open cat food container over Tom's dish.

"Well, you know how it is in this world today, when one receives a letter from someone out of the blue; it pays to do a little research before forming an alliance of any sort." I tell him, and accent the 'someone out of the blue' phrase. Tom repeats one of his loud meows and I dump the food into his dish without further hesitation. Silence on the phone line makes me ask "Are you still there?"

"Yes, yes, still here, it is a good idea and I do understand." He responds.

« »

She doesn't remember me at all I think as I answer her question. No wonder she hasn't contacted me sooner, she received a letter from a total stranger.

Now what? Should I tell her when we met and make her feel badly for forgetting? Or should I move on to the reason for the letter; I'll opt for the latter.

"Sarah, I know your reputation for thoroughness in research; I've seen your articles on the network plus the commentary from those who've worked with you. And I've read your book; quite useful to a beginner like me." I tell her in sincerity.

"I play at genealogy, but really don't have the time or methods to conduct the research as it should be done. That's why I decided to contact you and beg for your assistance," I say and wait to hear her response, but there's only silence on her side so I forge ahead.

"I wonder if you'd like to make a trip over," I ask her. "I know this may seem a little sudden, but there are documents here in the family library that I believe you might find interesting. I'd pay for the ticket of course and you are more than welcome to stay in our home with my father and me, there's plenty of room." I stop as I realise my rambling resembles a child trying to convince a parent of a field trip. I've surprised myself, since I'd thought the trip necessary but hadn't made up my mind before this call.

« »

He's talked on for a good minute. I hear all of what he's saying, but can't believe this man wants me to drop everything, leave my home and stay with not one, but two total strangers who are paying my fare to the U.K.

I believe him to be sincere by the tone of his voice and for some reason I feel comfortable that indeed, he shares a legitimate interest in his family. *He must be serious to have read my book* I think. But still, it's a bit much and I start to shy away from a hasty decision.

"Mr. Smith, I appreciate your offer," I tell him, "but I will need to think it over and give you my answer tomorrow, if you don't mind." I try to sound convincing when everything in me is saying Stop! You don't know this person, are you crazy?

"Thomas." I hear him say, but don't understand.

"What?" I question him.

"Please call me Thomas, Mr. Smith is my father to my friends."

I can't help but smile at his correction.

"Okay Thomas, thank-you very much for your offer, I will think about it and contact you tomorrow."

"Very good Sarah, thank-you for calling and I look forward to hearing your answer. By the way, hope your cat received his dinner."

"How did....you heard?"

"Yes, we have a similar resident here at Highbridge who regularly lets us know what time it is." He relates with a laugh.

"Yes Thomas, he's been taken care of and you're welcome. Good bye."

I put the phone down thinking, *that wasn't too bad* then amaze myself later by starting to sort out reasons pro and con for the trip as I ready for bed.

What name did he use, Highbridge? Must be a small town; how uncomfortable it would be if I'm tucked up into some cramped room under the eaves with a leaky thatched roof.

I like cosy, just not the leaky roof part. And what about sharing a bathroom with a family I don't know; not on my list of favorites either. I just don't know if I'll be comfortable enough to relax and concentrate on the job.

I remember my spur-of-the-moment trip to see Brian while he studied at Oxford. He'd called often during his months away but it was torture to be apart; holidays were the worst without him.

By Memorial Day I couldn't stand it and made a silent vow to earn enough money to see him by the 4th of July. I did it by working part time at the book store and doing a manuscript for a friend with just enough time to finish the draft, collect my pay and pack.

I called Brian an hour before stepping onboard at LaGuardia and he swept me up into his arms at Heathrow. We had so much catching up to do and luckily he had a two week summer break.

He took me all over London to show me the sights and we stayed in his apartment near the university after he charmed the landlady with one of his smiles and financed a dinner out for her and her husband.

Brian's roommate left to spend the holiday with his father so we pushed the twin beds into one to spend our long nights together.

Goodbye was hard after those weeks and the downside of the visit, but his studies were finished before Christmas and we never parted again except...I stop myself and concentrate on the present.

I reach to switch off the bedside lamp and pull the down-filled comforter over me. Mr. Smith's...Thomas' voice and his laughter about cats echoes in my mind.

Suddenly I sit straight up...good grief, it's Thomas—Brian's roommate. We met briefly as he left the apartment for his holiday. "Why didn't I remember him before?" I moan and fall back on my pillow.

"He must think I'm a total ditz." I say before sinking back into sleep.

Tom settles down at my feet again, ever tolerant of my unpredictable behavior.

I've finished the last of my research list in my husband's line today and feel a little weary as I close the computer for the evening. After 24 hours I still can't come to a decision about Thomas' offer and I need an objective opinion from someone outside my family.

Mom would be opposed; 'women just don't go running off to a foreign country on a whim' she told me when I went to see Brian. Besides Mom and Dad are in St Thomas on the vacation of their dreams and I really don't want to take their minds off just having fun.

Judy! She'll give it to me straight I think with a smile and turn off the desk lamp. In the living room I sink into my favorite, overstuffed yard-sale chair and push speed dial #3 on my cell. It takes just two rings for Judy to answer.

"Sarah, I was just thinking of you. How are you, what's new?" I hear what sounds like dance music behind her.

"Hi, is this a bad time? I can call later or tomorrow..." I offer.

"No, this isn't a bad time at all; just working out a little. Let me turn off the treadmill, grab a towel and get my water bottle," she begs. "I'm trying to shape up after gaining a couple of pounds and get a jump on the Thanksgiving and Christmas food coming on."

"I hate you." I jest.

Judy laughs at me. "Have you called to abuse me or is there another reason in mind here?"

"I have an invitation to fly to the U.K., all expenses paid, to do some genealogy work," I answer.

"Whoa girl, you're so unlucky. What's the problem?"

"It's an old friend of Brian's."

"Oh...oh." I hear her and my heart falls.

"What do you mean "Oh...oh"? Do you think I should do it?" I ask.

"Is it that simple or do you have misgivings?" She answers with another question.

"Of course I have misgivings; I wouldn't be me without them, you of all people should know that. Just tell me what you think."

"Okay, okay, how good a friend was he of Brian's and what do you know about him?" She asks.

"I didn't even remember him until last night when I started thinking over our conversation. We did meet once; he was Brian's roommate at university. He probably thinks I'm the ditziest woman he's ever talked to."

"Well, you don't know that Sarah and besides, he's looking for someone who's good at genealogy and you're excellent at it. He's offered to fly you over there with what I would imagine is a round-trip ticket, put you up in his family home, feed you and generally put up with you and pay you; have you discussed money yet? What else is there to know?" A long silence follows.

"Sarah, are you still there?" Judy asks.

"Yes, I'm still there...here. I guess when you say it like that, there isn't anything else to know...except, how am I going to handle this?" I bite my lip waiting for her reply.

"Look Sarah, you've been through some tough stuff in past years...more than some folks get in their whole life. But you've come through as a survivor and done well. What could be any worse than what you've already experienced? I say take the chance to break out of your rut and do this. You're up to date on your work at this point, so no problem there. Do you want me to come down, I could be there tomorrow?" She offers.

"No, no, that's not necessary, you're right as usual. I'm a survivor and I'm not 20-something anymore...I can do this." I say it more for my own benefit than for Judy's. "I'm going to call him back tonight and say 'yes' for this trip." I smile at my declaration.

"Alright--that's my Sarah. Call me when you get over there and let me know you're safe. Have you told your Mom and Dad?" She asks.

"I will, maybe after I get there," I hedge and hear her groan.

"I'm telling you right now if they call me, I'm a terrible liar and will probably blab your location and story as soon as they ask," Judy confesses.

"No, seriously I will call them before I leave and tell all," I promise her.

"Ok, I'm jumping back on the treadmill, don't forget to enjoy the trip and don't just work all the time you're there."

"I will, I mean I will enjoy and I won't just work; and Judy, thanks for being you."

"What's that supposed to mean?" She fakes obstinence, but continues, "See you when you get back."

I lean back in the chair and find Thomas's number next; his phone rings several times until his recording comes on.

"Darn." *Why can't he just answer while I'm still revved up from Judy's pep talk?* I think and leave a short message.

I'm off to the bedroom to strip off my wrinkled clothes for a shower and Tom settles into the resulting heap for a nap.

Just as I pour shampoo, the cell phone rings and I quickly wrap up in a towel to sprint to the bedside stand.

"Hello.'

"Hello, Sarah?" Of course it's Thomas and I stand here dripping into the carpet.

"Thomas, could you please hold a minute, I've just popped out of the shower and need to grab a robe."

"Oh, a...sure, no problem, I'll wait." He answers.

Oh boy, why did I give him that visual? I quickly dry off and put on an oversize robe before picking up the phone.

"Thank-you for returning my call, Thomas."

"No problem," he answers, "I hope this is good news?"

"Well, yes, I would like to come over and see the documents and records you mentioned. It's rare to get such an opportunity and I think it might be very good to gauge what can be found for your family's history."

"Wonderful. I'll send the flight tickets to you and you can arrange the dates to suit your schedule." He continues to carry on without interruption. "Now for expenses I'm sending you a credit card for incidentals, tips, meals and the like. Is your passport in order? It's rather an involved process if it isn't."

"Whoa there Thomas, stop just a minute please," I halt his momentum. "We haven't even discussed money yet for my time. I charge $250 per work hour plus any expenses connected with travel or supplies in relation to the research. I'll be sending you a contract for your signature; please sign and return it electronically; and may I have your email address?" I ask finally.

"Of course; sorry for the uncontrolled input there," he says then continues at the same speed. "It's just that this is important to me and I'm so pleased you've decided to accept.

"Your quote is reasonable and acceptable and you have my verbal agreement to those provisions, but I will sign the contract and send it back.

"Please let me know as soon as your arrival schedule is set so that I can arrange for someone to meet you." He pauses and I cease the window to reply.

"I'll have the airline send you the itinerary Thomas," I finally interject. "Thank-you for this, I look forward to getting started."

"Right then Sarah, talk to you soon." And with that I hear the click of his phone as he ends the call.

What is the expression? The plan is afoot or something? I can't help but smile and look down at Tom who now lays on the bed with feet in the air, sound asleep.

"Tom! What will I do with you?"

Chapter 2 – Plan's Afoot

This morning I called Delta and asked how to transport a cat on vacation to the U.K.: implant chip, rabies shot, a carrier meeting international standards, vet confirmation of health certificate, all endorsed by 'a necessary authority' whomever that is, was their answer.

Tom lays curled up comfortably at my feet "I hope you appreciate this." I tell him. The Vet's office luckily confirmed that Tom received his rabies booster two months ago and they will sign the necessary papers.

"Hi Mom, how are you two doing after your big adventure?" I ask her as I make my lunch.

"Sarah, it's so good to hear your voice. Dad and I were just talking about you." Gloria exclaims.

They surprised me last month by taking their first vacation in years in St. Thomas. It was so much fun to hear them on speakerphone, interrupting each other and laughing as I hadn't heard them in years. They must have had fun, they called me just once to let me know their return date and flight time. Quite a change from their first two years of retirement spent micromanaging my life and pressuring me to go back to school.

"We're fine and glad to be back but, after St Thomas it feels a little quiet, know what I mean?"

"Vacations can do that; it's the post fantasy letdown. Are you still looking for condos?"

"Well, yes and no; that's what we wanted to talk to you about." Gloria ends cautiously.

"What's going on Mom?"

"Well, there's no easy way to say this I guess...we're moving to St Thomas."

"You're serious? Wow. What in the world prompted all this?" I sit down, somewhat in shock.

"Oh Sarah, we loved St Thomas; the people, the countryside, the island life, the shopping and the way everyone lives there. We looked at our lifestyle here and remembered how we said we'd live our dreams before we were too old. It's a huge change for us and for you I'm afraid."

"Mom, I think it's wonderful."

"You do?" The relief in her voice comes through the phone. "Oh it's so good to hear you say that." I hear my Dad, Pat, in the background.

"We were afraid you'd try to talk us out of it and we just didn't know if we could say no, if you really needed us to stay."

"I would never do that to you guys," I tell Mom, "I'm a big girl now and besides there are airplanes down there every day and they run north as well." I joke to reassure them both. "We can see each other once in a while and talk as often as we want; it's okay."

"Come over tonight for dinner," Mom invites, "we'll tell you how all this came about and what our plans are, okay? We're on our way out to run some errands and should be back around 4 pm. I'll pick up something good so we don't have to cook."

"Sounds great; I'll be there. Congratulations."

I realise as I hang up the phone I haven't told them my news about the trip, which means I'll have to tell them face to face tonight. But I have the advantage with the advent of their bombshell. How can they disapprove my little trip after preparing to completely change their entire lifestyle?

When I pull up to their house in Belleglade later, every light in the house is on and music drifts down the street. I step out of the car and recognize some big band song playing. I knock on the door then walk in and watch with fondness as they dance. When the song ends, Dad plants a kiss on Mom's upraised face and they both look up in surprise as I clap my hands.

"Nice moves you two." I hug them both.

"Thank-you," Dad says as he blushes, "We practiced on vacation; not bad for an old man, eh?"

"Not bad at all Dad." I step back to look at them and notice they have wonderful tans and a twinkle in their eyes that wasn't there before.

"You both look fantastic"

"We feel fantastic; it's amazing what a little change can do for people." Mom says and moves to a bottle on the side table to offer me a glass.

"Champagne?" I ask.

"Yes, we wanted you to help us toast our new life." Dad fills the glass and brings it to me.

I hesitate slightly and take what I hope is an imperceptible deep breath.

"In that case Mom, Dad, I have something to tell you. I've been offered a temporary genealogy job in the U.K. and I'm leaving day after tomorrow."

I watch their faces as they struggle to understand me then Dad finally says with a smile to Mom, "Guess we all have news to share; come sit down and tell us about it."

"I received a letter a few weeks ago from a Thomas Smith in London asking if I could do some research for him. Apparently his family history is quite cloudy and he's been searching for more information on his great grandfather. He offered travel costs as well as free room and board at his family's home in North Yorkshire and didn't even pause when I informed him of what I expected in terms of pay." I tell them and take a sip of the champagne to give them both time to consider my news.

"What do you know about him?" Mom asks.

Dad chimes in, "Is this guy reputable; have you done your homework?"

"Turns out he was a best friend of Brian's at college, but I didn't remember him at first," I answer them. "Yes, I did an internet search and found several articles on him and his father who by the way, recently stepped down as CEO of a family-established company named Smith Imports Limited in London. Thomas left as the company's Director of Marketing at the same time and I'm not sure what he's doing at present."

"Did you check for any legal problems in their backgrounds?" Mom asks.

"Yes, I called a friend of mine who works for the CIA and has connections in Europe. There's nothing on record for any members of their family and in fact, though they're not aristocracy, they seem to be a well-respected family. The company is over 100 years old and founded by Thomas' grandfather."

Both are silent for a few moments and I wait, barely breathing, in readiness for more questions.

"Who do you know in the CIA?" They ask in unison.

"If I told you, I'd have to kill ya," I jest, "but seriously, I can't tell you a name; it's a former high school acquaintance of mine."

"What if you get over there and just can't stand either this Thomas or his family?" My Mom always searches for emergencies.

"The ticket is round trip and I'm not averse to telling either of them that I need to head home at any given time, but I could use you for an excuse if I need one." They both agree and plan a regular check-in call.

"Now let's have that toast." Dad says as we lift our glasses, "Here's to good luck in each of our new ventures."

We walk to the kitchen to discuss plans over dinner. I've had a nagging question in the back of my mind since first hearing of their move and decide this is my opportunity.

"If you don't mind my asking, I pretty much know what you two earned as teachers; are you sure you can comfortably make this move?"

Mom looks at Dad and asks "Pat, shall we tell her?" He nods.

"We've been holding on to your college fund on the chance that in later life you might want to return and finish up. Remember how I kept asking you about that?" Mom asks.

I remember it well as pressure, but won't tell them that now.

"We, rather your father, has been investing the money over the last 20 years and it's evolved into quite a hefty amount—well over the one million mark." She says casually and sets her glass down as I look up from my cheesecake with wide eyes.

"Good grief. Remind me to put you two in charge of my meager savings account."

"We were lucky," Dad explains, "we and a little social media company, not so small anymore. One of my colleagues at school had the foresight to see its value and discussed it with me. Those opportunities don't come often and it may have been foolish, but I took the chance. It could have gone either way, but it went our way and we thank God every day that it did because it's enabled us to live our dream in St. Thomas..."

"And to give you your share," Mom adds then holds up her hand when I start to protest.

Dad continues, "We know Brian had little insurance when he passed, few young people can afford decent insurance and we didn't blame him for that. He found himself in a sudden and unfair circumstance and after he realised he wouldn't be around much longer he told us he worried about your well-being. Your mother and I had been investing your unused tuition money and offered to keep it going so that it would be there should you ever need it. Brian was visibly relieved and he passed knowing you'd be taken care of."

Dad comforts me with a hug when he sees the tears in my eyes.

"We wanted to do this for you and for Brian," he says. "We loved him as the son we didn't have, Sarah." We stand together for a little while until the wave of emotion passes.

27

"I understand now Dad." I look at them with new respect. "Thanks for what you've done, both of you. I know you could have lived in more comfort over the years and had I known, I would never have held you to such a promise. But because it's what Brian wanted, I will accept the original amount..." It was my turn to stop their protests.

"The original amount you set aside and no more." I repeat. They see I won't budge and agree to my decision.

The hours have flown by and it's 11p.m. as I drive home. *This evening is the stuff novels are written about* I think to myself, but it happened in my family's living room and I say a little prayer that God will protect them both in their new journey.

Chapter 3 Highbridge Homecoming

*E*yes open; sun up, *computer alarm going off* my sleep-fogged mind reminds me.

"Right." I remark aloud and order both legs over the edge of the bed—<u>now</u>.

The computer mimics Big Ben and finishes up the hour as I sit listening. Always reminds me of coming to London years ago with Dad on a lark and hearing Ben's deep tones for the first time. There was nothing like it at home in the country and I stopped in mid-step to pull on his hand. We listened together as people flowed around us in their rush to work that morning, veritable rocks in the stream we were; a good memory.

Enough—get to it! I shake myself from the memory and make my way down the hall to the bathroom for a hot shower.

The flat's chill cools the soles of my bare feet and I look out the window to see the fog just clearing as the morning sun beats it back. Good, no rain today, no blasted brollies I think as I reach into the shower to turn on the water. Stepping in, I have a sudden wakeup as the hot water turns hotter and I adjust it down a bit.

A quick dry off, shave and a splash of aftershave then it's to the closet.

Conservative dark suits line the cedar walls. Shirts hang in order of varying colors from the often-required white to the less-stodgy blue, pinstripe and even checkered. That last was a gift from Lydia last Christmas. She stopped by early with a bottle of wine and a package wrapped to the nines; she always had a gift for wrapping.

I grab the checkered shirt then team it up with a tie and dark suit for the day. Not too traditional as I look in the mirror, but not so far over the edge the Board members will frown and I recall the several scheduled meetings regarding import lists today.

After taking final inventory of wallet and keys, I head for the kitchen and cross to the front entry to collect the London Times and USA Today from the doorstep. The hallway is empty I note as I straighten up; all tourists have left the building. Learning last week that many of these flats have been acquired by rental agents was a shock. Certainly fortunate Dad thought to secure this flat for our use or my weekday stays wouldn't be half as comfortable as they've been since university. I notice his overcoat is missing from the hook by the door; he's probably already at the office.

Overhead lights supplement the daylight filtering from the small window into the cramped galley and soon the teakettle is up and the steamy brew warms my cup. I gingerly retrieve a toasty bagel and lather cream cheese over it then sit down to the morning papers.

Economy in tough shape right now I think and read the stock market reports for the latest. This recession has bollixed every aspect of trade for months and the banks here and abroad are not helping. Blasted newspapers fanning the flame with their coverage; commodities dropped almost overnight last year as the masses began to prepare for a full-out crash in the market.

Dad's been under serious pressure with it, and I look up from the paper upon thinking of him; high blood pressure isn't something he needs at his age.

Dishes to the sink for cleanup and thoughts of the letter I sent earlier in the week to Brian's widow come to mind. *Blast.* Did I do this wisely...contacting a woman who probably doesn't even remember me? I store the dishes away in the cupboard and walk to the lounge.

It's been ten years since I first met her and I think of her as she was then; that curly auburn hair and blue eyes, she was something. At first I envied my friend Brian's good fortune but no question in my mind they were meant for each other. He was a lucky man. Well...ultimately not so lucky; cancer snuffed out a good husband for Sarah and my friend.

I remember how people ribbed us about being twin Smiths at university. Class seats were alphabetically scheduled during that year and we became best friends early-on, even chipping in on the apartment off-campus. I sent my sympathy to Sarah on Brian's passing but heard nothing in return.

I don't make a habit of doing things without thorough consideration, I remind myself, and pick up my briefcase. But the buck stops here with me as the last of our family's line and neither I nor father can spare the time for the research required. Rediscovering Sarah's book Genealogy for the Beginner on my bookshelf last week seemed a sign. For some reason the idea of hiring "an outsider" versus someone local seems logical. It might assure more privacy in case any "skeletons" turn up, though fat chance of anything that exciting in our family.

I close the flat's door and turn to summon the lift. A hasty tourist already on the car pushes the button then looks up, startled to see me jump in just as the door begins to close.

The street is alive with the noise of rush hour traffic. I breathe in the cool dampness of another chilly morning as I head east and quickly merge with the crowd for Gloucester station two brisk blocks away. I consciously walk a quicker pace to elevate my heart rate while some slow movers carry coffee or breakfast to eat as they walk. The scent of warm food mixed with an infrequent whiff of perfume from the shop girl ahead of me exercises my sense of smell quite pleasantly.

The train pulls in on time and I board to use ride-time for a brief review of the first meeting's notes then walk the short distance from the train to Smith Imports' venerable granite façade. I'm regularly reminded of the hands-on nature of this challenging business; not one which can be run remotely and I will spend as many hours as needed to lighten the load on Dad's shoulders.

"Good morning Margaret" Father's assistant of many years sits in the outer office and I pause a moment to look at her. Somehow she always manages to stay together in the most trying of times and this is no exception. She is quite the lady with her silver streaked auburn hair just so and brown eyes sparkling.

"Dad in there?" I ask and cross to his office.

"Oh yes, he's been here since before I arrived sir and you know how early that is."

"Yes, I probably do, but we know why don't we?

"Indeed we do sir."

"Thank-you Meggs." I knock lightly at Stephen's door before entering.

"Hello Dad, how are you this morning?" The man I see at the desk has changed in the past year. The lines around his eyes have grown deeper, his hair changed from sporadic graying at the temples to a light gray over most of his head.

He does take very good care of himself with daily exercise, an occasional boxing match at the gym and long walks on the moors at the family Estate in North Yorkshire on weekends. But his appearance this morning admits to the obvious; this year has been unreasonably hard.

"There's something I wanted to discuss with you, if you have time." I remark and sit in one of the old traditional Phillip Morris chairs he refuses to part with.

"Thomas, you know I always have time for you," He smiles and puts down his pen, "but I need a word before you begin, please."

I sit back and turn my full attention to him.

"There's something you should know." Stephen rises from his chair and walks to the window then slowly turns to face me.

"I've been asked to step down as Chair and I'm seriously considering it."

"Father, you can't be serious. Who asked this—who engineered this?"

"I received the official letter this morning by messenger." He picks up the letter from his desk to bring it to me.

I read it and see the signatures of eight board members, a majority of the vote, requesting him to step-down due to 'age constraints'. This Company was founded over 100 years ago by Charles Smith, my grandfather, as a means to supply the military during the war. Today's commodities, paper and plastics, are sold to the building industries very successfully. My father's efforts through the recession kept the Company in the black; their decision to remove a direct descendant of the founder is incomprehensible.

"Did you have any idea it was coming?"

"No, I did not. I've noticed a lull in phone calls from board members and suppose I should have taken a clue from that." He sits down at his desk to continue.

"I don't know that it's a bad idea son. I'm not my usual self at this point." Seeming to sense the worry in my face he adds, "I mean I'm beginning to feel the fight isn't worth it anymore."

I've never heard him make such a statement. Seconds creep by until I ask "What do you mean Dad?"

He smiles. "You know how long I've been at this and there are other things in life besides the import business. I'd like to live at the Estate again fulltime and give it the attention it deserves. I think it could pay for itself again with a good farm supervisor and I have other ideas too."

"What ideas?" I'm in awe of this man who sits before me proposing ways to change his entire life.

"I want to build a mill on Copper Swift. That old stream has run strong through our property and never been low. I think we could do well with our own line of stone-milled flours and give the village a boost with some new jobs." He turns back to the window and gazes at the sky before continuing.

"Your mother always wanted to help bring jobs to the village and I forged ahead with this company, too blind to see the wisdom in what she was saying." He remains quiet for a few seconds then turns to me.

"That's where I'm at son, what do you think?"

"Is there enough money to sustain such a large undertaking, Dad?"

"What's enough?" he quips. "I've been pretty close to the line all my life; never squandered the odd pound, always putting it somewhere it would be safe to grow. I think I've managed to keep the employees who work for us paid their fair share and I don't think I've shorted the family's needs too badly, do you?

I remember the family gatherings on the lawn, the trips to Brighton beach in the summer, the college tuition and support until I received my certificate.

"No Dad, you've done just fine by me and this company."

"I do recognize that we can't continue to support a house the size of Highbridge in these times." He tells me. "The family fortune has seriously eroded, not drastically enough that we have to sell off land, but it is a wake-up call for action. We have enough assets to invest in some new, well thought out endeavors and I believe the ones I've mentioned may result in a rebuilding of the Estate's trust funds and some needed support for our neighbors."

"If this is what you want I'll support your decisions Dad."

"Oh, you most definitely are part of it my boy. I want you to shadow me during the phase-out here, make sure everything's by the book so to speak and help me ensure that the Smith name is kept right where it belongs as the respected founder of this company. I want to retain a seat on the Board after stepping down, just to keep a finger on the company's pulse. I have fifty percent of the company's stock between your mother's shares and mine; with yours added, I can still have a say in what's what."

He finishes with a flurry and leans back against the window sill. "Now, tell me where you are in all this. Do you want to take over my position and be married to this place for the next forty years the way I've been?"

"I never thought of it like that." I say upon reflection. "I respect the history of this company and what it's meant to our family. I've enjoyed the challenges too, but I especially enjoy working at your side." I tell him and Dad circles the desk to stand before me as I continue.

"I think it was all about learning the business from you, being your right hand man, but mostly just being here. I don't think it will be the same without you, so I have to think seriously about this."

"Alright Thomas, take the next twenty-four hours; if you decide you want to give the Chairman position a run, I'll support you with the Board and make sure every opportunity is given for your appointment. On the other hand, if you decide not to follow in the old man's footsteps, I have another proposal for you." I see a twinkle in his eyes.

"What's that?" I ask.

"I'll need a right hand man at Highbridge; someone who can handle the farm's management, hire and fire where needed, find the right people to bring the best, progressive new farm practices our way."

"Dad, I know very little about farming; I was young when we did operate one and they didn't include farm practices in my business courses."

"Now, hold on, that's not all son. I need someone to supervise the building of the mill, find us the best experienced workers and the best of grains. All of that has to be packaged, marketed and properly licensed. Then there's working with the locals. Big enough job for you Mr. Business?" Dad teases me.

I realise an unexpected feeling of excitement at his suggestions. The Estate is rich with our history; my grandfather Charles was born there and I've stood on its edges too long. If I can contribute to its future, why not take this chance to do so? It isn't really a question is it? I smile as I realise my direction has become clear, my decision is already made with no further need of hesitation.

"I'll go with you Dad and we'll do it together. I know you probably see a mix of happiness and amazement on my face at an unusually quick decision, but for some reason, I truly feel it's the right thing in my heart."

We share a rough hug with thumps on the others' back until Meggs opens the door.

"What's going on in here?" she demands, half-smiling.

"We're embarking on a new adventure," Stephen exclaims. "Would you like to come along?"

"Oh Mr. Smith, I haven't had an adventure for a very long time," she laughs, "it sounds intriguing."

"Right then. Thomas, fill Meggs in on the particulars while I go on to the Board meeting. Join me at the meeting when you finish here and we'll hammer out the details later at dinner."

Margaret and I listen as Stephen walks briskly down the hall whistling a marching theme from a popular WWII movie. We look at each other then burst into laughter.

"Oh my, is Mr. Smith alright?" She asks.

"Meggs, he hasn't been this right in a long time. Please sit down and let me tell you about it and...offer you a job."

《 》

North Yorkshire is in fine shape this morning I think as I drive the last five miles home. It's mid-October, the leaves have changed to their brightest hues and are beginning to drop in earnest. The air is clear and crisp and sunlight filters through the trees to the winding tarmac, making the surface appear lattice-worked.

I finished up this morning at Smith Imports and closed my door for the last time; it was much easier than I thought it would be. I've enjoyed most aspects of the business beyond the inflated politics of the Board and their deceit, but Dad's question 'are you prepared to give the next 40 years to the company?' was on the mark. I don't want that even if it is tradition and marvel at the wake-up call he gave me; no way could I ignore it.

I drive in at the familiar gate posts and continue up the brick-lined drive, a sight I've loved since I arrived from Kent with my parents at the age of four. Grandfather Charles fell ill and requested their help; my Dad Stephen and mum Irene came immediately to take on his duties for the Estate in a temporary arrangement then later sold our home to stay after the cancer took him.

That was a long time ago and much has changed in our family and in the world; Windows, I think and another window to step through with the building of the mill and revival of the farm.

In truth, the old Estate money left by grandfather began to decrease most through the past recession. Dad responded well to prevent a complete collapse of the Trust, but the warning signs were clear and we both realise the need to diversify and make the place pay for itself again. I don't think he knows how much I love and respect his actions and service to our obligations. Not many would do what he's done in the last month, let alone a lifetime.

I glance to the left of the drive and notice the site for the mill has already been cleared beside the Copper Swift, visible from the house as Dad stipulated. The branding of the mill is so important I think and wonder how the 'Copper Swift Mill Company' would sound to Dad. It has a nice ring and I'll bring it to him at the first opportunity.

A lot of happy days were spent beside that swift stream while I was growing up; fishing, catching tadpoles and salamanders under the rocks on shore; all high on my list at ten years of age, and it makes me smile even now.

Dad stayed in London a lot after mother died and I remember those dark days as well. Now the stream, like an old and steady friend, waits to greet me again and I look forward to spending time at its side.

To the right of the drive, the familiar hillside rises high, covered by forest made up of ash, beech and maple, its fall colors wash the sky with reds and yellows. A stone wall separates the drive from the rise to prevent slides during the winter months and its crevices harbor ferns and ivy from the forest floor. A fence line around the forest sweeps up and behind the Estate house separating the rough meadows from the kept grounds on one side and the forest on the other; both provide a green, wooded backdrop for the house.

41

Ahead and over the rise, Highbridge comes into view with its gray granite walls shining almost silver in the afternoon sun. It's been here since 1887 and I appreciate anew its modest architecture compared to other estates in the area. I remember little of our old house before moving here; two generations born here and the lifestyle provided makes me feel very blessed indeed.

Parking just past the large stone steps leading to the entryway, I turn off the ignition and reach into the back seat to retrieve a present picked up at Harrods's in London before leaving this morning. Clothing and belongings have already been sent ahead, so with the crunch of gravel under my feet I make my way toward the house.

I pause and stop for a moment to listen to the sound of distant mowing and breath in the scent of sweet grass. The trees on the other side of the drive are full of finches flitting here and there, the red leaves of the copper beech shine in welcome under the noonday sun. I remember the tree as I first saw it at four years of age. Grandfather Charles planted it upon my birth and look at it now, forty feet or more straight up.

I stand wrapped in nostalgia until I hear "Well are you coming in?" from behind me. Turning toward the familiar voice, I take the steps two at a time and embrace Emily, our housekeeper of many years, who was both my nemesis as a teenager and confidant/advisor during Father's absences in London.

"Ems, how are you?" I laugh as she struggles to keep her composure but never the less hugs back before I turn her loose.

"I'm just fine sir. You're looking rather puny, what are you eating these days, yogurt and cheerios?"

"First of all, what is this 'sir' business and secondly, you don't have to worry about what I'm eating as if I'm still at university." I laugh and give her another hug as she attempts to protest gives in since at a little over five foot tall to my six, she hasn't the strength to win anyway.

"Now Thomas, you know it's proper to include 'sir' as you've grown up and hold position in the world now."

"Emily, I will never hold so much position here or in the world that you won't always be like a second mother to me, so stop this nonsense and continue to call me Thomas whenever you like—please." Then I release her.

"Alright Sir...I mean, Thomas." She glances around to make sure no one has overheard. "Now please come in, your father's in the library. Cook has made a good lunch for you both and I'll just go tell him you've arrived."

"That sounds wonderful, tell Jamie I'm starving." By the time I pick up the present I placed on the railing, Emily is already halfway down the long hall in her typical hurried pace.

"The house looks great Emily" I call as I step into the entry hall large enough to hold a ten foot huntsmen's table grandfather used for hunting parties years ago. The hall leads into the great room with its fireplaces centered on north and south walls. Beyond to the back of the house I can just see the sun reflecting off the chandeliers of the dining room, large enough to serve a group of forty if need be. The well-stocked library is off to the left of the great room, with its book collections from all the house's residents, past and present and it's into this doorway I step first to check in with Dad.

I find him sitting in a favorite chair by one of two high windows, surrounded by books on the floor, on the tables, beside and in front of him, completely immersed in the one in hand.

"Dad, what's all this? Looks like you have enough reading here to spend the winter."

"Ah Thomas, so glad you made it son." He shuts the book with a firm hand and rises to meet me.

"It's research for the farm and for the mill, now don't get upset," as I begin to protest, "I'm just doing this for my own benefit, so that I can at least take part in the planning with some knowledge base. You know I don't come to a meeting without being prepared." We share a rough hug then pull out chairs to sit down at the large oak table in the middle of the room.

"It's just that I've been so immersed in the import business, it's a long time since I learned anything new and I want to make a good show of it."

"Dad, give yourself some credit, I know how well-prepared you are and wouldn't expect anything less. I just hope you're going to share your reviews with me until I get up to speed."

"Of course, in fact, why don't we decide right now to meet at least once a week?"

"Dad, what do you think of the name, 'The Copper Swift Mill Company' for our new brand?"

"I never considered it, always thought it would be named with either 'Smith' or 'Highbridge' or some of both." He mulls it over some more, saying it out loud a couple of times.

"The Copper Swift Mill Company...I like it. Strong on the tongue; memorable I would even say. I think your idea is a bully one Thomas. I'll leave it to you to apply for the copyright and we hope that won't run into any snags, but to my knowledge there is no other company named as such."

"Then it's my first initiative and I'll file by the end of the week for the rights," I tell him. "We'll just hope for the best, if not, we'll come up with something even better." I feel my smile grow with excitement, knowing we can guide our own ship instead of running everything through the board first. I believe this will be quite a good journey.

"Let's eat!" Dad announces. "I hear Jamie has a delicious lunch ready for us." We walk out to the patio on the west end of the house overlooking the valley and the Copper Swift mill site. Sandwiches of sliced roast beef on wheat bread, topped with lettuce, cucumber, tomato and spicy mustard have already been plattered and brought to the table; potato salad cold from the fridge and a dessert, crème cake with lemon filling sit nearby.

When we finish, Dad and I push back from the table to take a walk, descending to the rear gardens by way of the terraces at the back of the house.

"John's still handling the vegetables and flowers?" I ask and notice the neatly groomed rows of late season table vegetables; rutabagas, carrots, cabbages and the like.

"Yes, he's stubborn that way, wants to make sure all is in order. He was hired by your mother as head gardener many years ago as you know, but with her death and my disinterest in such things, John completely took over the gardens and supported the family's table. With his excellent care, the produce is way over what we use in the house and he sells to the Village grocery at wholesale; built up quite a nice little seasonal business."

"His determination reminds me of someone else I know." I shoot a glance in his direction in time to see Dad smile, knowing who his son refers to, before he continues.

"John's been here a long time but won't think of retirement, told me that I should bring it up if ever he starts flagging though. I do have a couple of youngsters from the Village come up once a week to help with the weeding and bending jobs, to keep his back in shape and I leave the boys' complete management up to him."

We walk up to the fence line of the forest then turn to lean on its wooden trestles and view the house and gentle slope of the valley.

"It's a fine view Dad."

"Yes, it's all there; two hundred and fifty acres, same as your grandfather left. I sometimes feel guilty I wasn't more present to oversee and direct its care; perhaps we wouldn't be in the financial situation we're in now if I had." he reflects. A gentle breeze stirs and rumples his hair and reminds him to continue.

"Ach, you can never see clear except when you're looking back and that's a fact. Your mother used to try to tell me, but I wouldn't have it. Age brings wisdom if you learn from your experiences and I often think of my dear Irene here on these family grounds. You know she never wanted to be here." His eyes are soft as he says it.

"She loved London and all it had to offer. She'd come from the country, fought to leave it for the city, but had to follow me back. Oh, she adjusted, of course and loved watching you run and play in the grass she'd loved as a child, She appreciated the fact that I brought her to her 'senses' as she put it and gave our son the chance to grow up healthy and happy. I believe she meant that."

He looks to me, "You've come along willingly haven't you, son? You're not here just to please your dad?"

"I'm here because of your courageous decision to strike out in another direction," I tell him. "I needed to do the same; you extended the invitation and my decision to follow feels right."

Dad sees the truth of what I'm saying in my eyes and replies with a resounding "Bully for you. Now, let's get back to the house so that you can get settled in. I had John put all your boxes in your old room; I hope that's what you'd planned? You can have your choice of any room, it's for sure no one else is using them." He laughs then puts his arm over my shoulders as we walk back down the hill toward home.

I go up to my old room at the back of the west hallway and throw open the door. Immediately I notice the lack of dust or cobwebs; Emily has been here cleaning again I acknowledge as I smile at its spotless condition. The dark blue drapes are open and the fading light of sunset makes the room slightly dusky. I flick on the ceiling light, noting dressers, chairs, bed, are all in their same places but a new desk and lamp sit at the window with access for the laptop I brought with me.

The boxes sent ahead are stacked on the opposite wall near the door; clothes are already unpacked, hung in the closet while others are folded in the chest of drawers. I'll need to adjust to having a housekeeper again, it's been a long time since anyone waited on me, I'm not especially comfortable with it anymore.

I sit down to let the quietness of the room soak in for a while. This room was always cooler in the morning and warmer at night, no central heat means the sun plays a role in how the house holds heat. But the back stairway to the kitchen is close at hand and I still like to hang about when meals are being prepared or sometimes raid for leftovers at night.

It afforded me a private entrance as a lad on the occasional late night out during breaks from university. I'm comfortable here, so no need to move elsewhere.

I reflect on the manner in which Stephen has kept the house up, grateful that the old leaded glass casements in the entire house now hold modern insulated frames to ward off drafts when the winds come off the northern moors in winter. As well, he's seen to it that all the fireplaces were relined and their chimneys repointed. He must have been thinking about moving back for some time before this happened.

Mother cared deeply about this house and gradually replaced what grandfather lost during his illness. Dad said that many of the home's furnishings mysteriously disappeared by the time they arrived. I remember him talking of Irene's passion for Estate sales; the village markets frequently had her bringing home interesting pieces. Sometimes a table or a chair said to have come from the Estate would without questions asked be repurchased, refurbished and placed back into service.

It's clear that things would have to get much worse before Dad would even consider selling any of the Estate's furnishings or land; that's just how I feel about it as well.

After a quick shower, I change into jeans and a loose-fitting jersey shirt, check my email then walk down the back stairs for what I hope will be a large dinner. It must be the country air, but I'm starving again. Delicious smells are coming from the kitchen and it feels good to be home; I've been traveling away too long.

Dad and I sit at the large kitchen table together and he seems interested in my story about Sarah.

"She'll stay here with us, I hope that will be acceptable Dad? I thought she could start with the various records in our library then branch out to other registries and sources as needed."

"I think that's a fine idea son. Of course any guest of yours is welcome, no need to ask, this is just as much your house as it is mine. I understand your curiosity about our forefathers; I've taken little interest since the company's welfare became my primary focus. My grandfathers' names, first or second were never discussed with me by Charles, except to say his father died in a war many years before I was born. Your mother used to encourage me to take an interest in our history, but it never worked. She said we were just as important as the royals, on a smaller scale of course and that our lineage needed to be put down on record for future generations. I'm proud of you for taking this step."

He sips his coffee then adds, "Let Emily know of your plans so she can ready a room for Miss Sandlin; make sure she's comfortable. We have a big day tomorrow with construction on the Mill, so now, if you have no objection, I'm off to my bed."

"I'm going there soon myself, good night Dad." He pushes out his chair and heads for the front stairs, but I linger with my coffee then carry it to the library where a wood fire is laid in the grate. I light it and sit in one of the side chairs to stare into the flames and soak up its warmth for a while.

The house is quiet, a few lights have been left on in the halls but everyone, family and staff, embraces the practice of turning out lights when leaving a room. Quite different from my life in London; not much to conserve in a small flat, except recycling of course.

Here on the Estate, waste glass, metal and paper is recycled through the Recycling Centre. John the gardener sees to the composting of the food waste for the garden although several pigs are still kept on the farm and receive food scraps from the kitchen, too. All in all I'm proud of what we're doing to live green for the planet.

Dad's proposal for the farm's management is a good idea, but all the knowledge I have I gleaned as a boy here; the periodic wheat and corn harvests, rotation of crops to enrich the soil, the sweet grass and corn stalks used for the stock in the winter months. Farming has changed with regulations and practices we never thought to consider before. They're environmentally-important but costly and I'm beginning to doubt that we can produce a profitable operation, given those various new conservation rules for the amount of land father owns.

I need to find someone expert on the subject and bring him in to have a look. I close the fire screen before going upstairs knowing I need to pursue this before we go too much further. Tomorrow I'll stop by the Village to see some old friends at the Grange.

"Good night sir." Bert, our inside 'man' says as he goes about his evening rounds.

"I've turned off the library lights Berty, the front entry halls too, so no need to go there. The library fire is just dying down and may need attention for the night." Berty, as he is affectionately known to family, came to work on the Estate as a young man straight from the Village school. He's stayed on to become a trusted and faithful member of our family for many years.

"Yes sir, I'll attend to it."

"Thank you Berty, good night."

Entering my room, I turn on the light at the desk to add a few notes to my calendar regarding the Grange visit and Sarah's arrival then fall into bed for a good night's sleep.

«»

Early this morning I park my car and walk up the familiar front steps of Highbridge house.

I remember all the times I've been here in the past to help Stephen and his wife Irene, too, when she was alive. They held wonderful employee celebrations for Smith Imports; I always admired them for the way they made everyone feel welcome at their events, greeting each guest personally, the house done up in style and the special plans for the children who were invited with their parents.

Stepping through today, Irene's death comes to mind after her critical heart attack. It left both Stephen and Thomas stunned and recovering for years. What a thrill it is to see them both come up to the surface, charting their new course and inviting me to join them at Highbridge as their assistant! I still hear Thomas's voice as he offered me the position those months ago.

London was exciting when I was younger, but it's become quite trying at my age and I do love the country so it's wonderful to be included. Details of our discussion on this arrangement are still fresh in my mind. Stephen at first insisted my salary level remain the same, but I was right to refuse since food and board will be provided. He finally gave in, but added that if ever I needed it, he hoped I would have no qualms about approaching him. It seems I'm retiring but opening a new phase in my life all at the same time.

Eager to see my friend Emily again, I take the hall to the back stairs down to the kitchen. It'll be exciting to see my new living quarters and all my things have been delivered so I shall get busy at putting them away today.

I spot Ems walking into the kitchen as I arrive. She quickly puts down a pile of towels to come and hug me enthusiastically.

"Margaret Jenkins. Wonderful to see you Meggs--how are you?" She holds me away to give me a going-over. "You look rested fit; ready to move in?"

"I am, are you ready for another person to mother-duck?" I ask her with a laugh.

"Oh I'm so happy you've decided to join us, I am indeed. Would you like a cup of coffee, or would you rather go up to see your room?"

"I think the room first maybe the coffee."

"The room it is, just let me get my load of towels, no reason not to take them up on the way, some are for your room anyway. I hope you don't have any trouble with stairs?"

"No, I'm very fit to walk them. Let me at least take half of those." She smiles and divides up the towels then together we walk the three flights to the third floor.

"Oh it's wonderful." I cry when we enter the apartment. The sitting room is complete with television, computer access, phone, even a small kitchenette with a fridge.

"So much more than expected," I exclaim as we go on through to the bedroom.

"It's just lovely, my favorite color of blue, however did you know?"

"Mr. Thomas told me. I believe there's a gift over there on the desk for you, he wanted you to have it when you arrived. All your boxes are on that wall; your bath is across the hall. My room is at the other end, my bath is opposite, so this one is exclusively yours."

"Thank you Emily, I so much appreciate your taking the time to bring me up here."

"Nonsense, you're a friend Meggs, don't forget that. Come down when you're ready and we'll have a sit-down with a cup of coffee, okay?"

"I will, just let me put some things away, say in about an hour?"

"No hurry, take your time, see you soon." Emily walks quickly down the hall with her towels as I turn to look around my new home then cross to the desk and pick up the gift box. I gently pull open the ribbon on its top; inside is a very nice watch with a note. I admire the watch and place it on my wrist then read:

"To Meggs;

A symbol of our gratitude, for your service at Smith's these many years. We hope that you continue to stay on with us and lend that same professionalism to our new endeavor."

Fondly - Thomas and Stephen.

Indeed, I've come home.

Chapter 4 Speechless

I sit in the Manchester International Airport's passenger pick-up area, having just successfully navigated Customs for both Tom and me. My wheeled luggage sits beside me, Tom is napping in his carrier and though weary from the time change and lack of sleep, I'm feeling pretty excited about this whole thing.

The airport "cast" has certainly changed since my last visit though and I watch three young men walk by with spiked hair in wild colors of red and purple. But it's exciting to see so many different people in one place and even the wait is enjoyable as I nibble on a sandwich then put some water in Tom's dish.

"We're running a little late," Thomas called a few minutes ago, "Traffic on the M1 is backed up due to an accident." I hope I recognize him from his picture on the computer I think nervously.

The weather's a little crisp, no humidity—heaven. I basically packed winter clothes with some lighter sweaters, which can be layered if needed but I've waited to purchase a heavier coat and a pair of Barbour wellies until after arrival.

Thomas told me the room heat in the house comes from fireplaces and electric heaters. My curiosity over what the house looks like is bugging me, but I imagine it small as so many houses built long ago are. Also in my imagination, plumbing either exists at minimum or isn't in good working order but I'm trying to be brave.

Families exit the terminal after connecting with those they love; my thoughts go to Mom and Dad. Their big move is planned for next week; I'm glad they decided to rent out their house versus selling which provides them a safety net if St. Thomas living doesn't pan out. They haven't completely lost their minds after all I think with a smile.

I examine the debit card Mom gave me before leaving; "For your share of the college fund dear." She said. They've always been supportive but I recognize the time has come to get on with my own life; this opportunity is just what I've needed.

A black Lexus pulls to the curb in front of me, both doors open and the driver approaches my luggage. I recognize Thomas as he steps out to walk up the sidewalk to greet me, hand extended. His attire is certainly different from his picture; Levi's, plaid shirt, morning shadow and hair blown over his forehead are quite a switch from the polished businessman in the newspaper.

"Hello Sarah." He shakes my hand vigorously, "How was your flight?"

"Uneventful, thank-you, not too crowded"

"Good, good." Then he looks at my single carry-on bag.

"That your luggage?" He bends over to peer into Tom's carrier.

"Let me guess—Tom. You are a big boy." Thomas remarks as he pokes a finger into the cage. Tom uses it to scratch behind one ear, as if to say he'd needed that for the last two hours.

Well, aren't you an instant pushover I think, as I watch my cat make a fool of himself for the man. Trust the animals to know who's on the level.

"Are you ready to go?" Thomas smiles at me and asks.

"Absolutely," I answer and follow him to the open door of the car where he introduces Bert, his driver. After stowing my bag with the pet carrier in the hatchback, we settle into the backseat to click our safety belts and Bert drives the car through the exit lanes.

The early morning haze lifts, with promise of a clear day for my first drive in the country. I note the city of Manchester has a beltway and of course everything on the road looks "backwards" to me. Thank heaven I'm being driven from the airport vs. renting a car to drive on the left myself...the thought makes me a bit queasy; either that or it's the fact I've arrived in what should be the middle of the night and feel like I've been up forever.

Thomas chats as we move through traffic, but I become aware he's looking at me now in expectation of something.

"What? I'm so sorry Thomas, what were you saying?"

"I asked if you were hungry, we might stop for a bite to eat." he says with concern, "but I can see you are somewhat time-weary. Tell you what, I'll give you a choice; stop for a bite, or we can motor on through to the house to raid the kitchen. Which do you prefer?" It didn't take a second to choose.

"Let's go through, I would welcome a peanut butter sandwich with a glass of milk at this point."

"Peanut butter it is." Then he smiles, "I haven't had one of those in years, it sounds delicious."

Bert drives like an expert through the traffic and I begin to notice the change in car types from those I'm used to seeing in the States. Most are European-made cars, the newer fuel-efficient models.

"How does this car do fuel-wise Bert?" I ask.

He beams at my inquiry, "We're getting around thirty-eight kilometers to the liter Miss; our other car at home outruns this by ten or twelve."

Our conversation then goes to comparison of roadways in the U.K. with those in Florida and I find there are similarities.

"We battle potholes here as well, Miss. The Department for Transport works with local government and there's a website for citizens to report not only potholes, but their ideas for road improvement."

"I wish we had something like that," I tell Bert. "We just call the mayor's office to complain."

"Unfortunately, if we did that, we'd be tagged as troublemakers," Thomas smiles, "though not publicly flogged, we wouldn't be well-thought of for evasion of the system. You know how we Brits love a good system."

"Well, actually I don't know, but I'll have fun finding out I suspect."

We pass the towns of Leeds and York; I almost ask how much further, but fear I'd sound like an impatient child, so refrain. We go to secondary roads then country lanes but before I think to ask again, Bert turns into a pair of stone gate heads on the right, with the name 'Highbridge' over them.

"Here we are, almost home now." Thomas reassures.

I note the landscape change from flat to gently rising hills; a forest rises on our right, farmland slopes away on our left. A lovely stream flows through the valley below where some sort of construction has begun in one area beside it.

"What's that?" I ask Thomas.

"It's our new venture, a mill for artisan flour and the like. I'll show you the plan when we get settled at the house, if you're interested."

"I would love to see it and walk down to the site, if that's possible." A welcome thought since I've been sitting the better part of the last eight hours. At this moment, the car comes over a gentle slope. I gape at what looks like a residence straight out of a fairy tale, the sun setting off a silver sparkle in its granite walls. There are numerous windows and more chimneys than I can count. With the large entryway and terraces surrounding the house, I am speechless. Thomas seems to notice my reaction.

"It's impressive when you get your first glance isn't it?"

"I'm...I didn't expect...I mean I didn't know..." I feel my face blush. "It's just that I thought it would be more modest in size..." That doesn't sound right either so I stop to collect myself before speaking again.

"I hope you don't have an aversion to big old houses that creak and sigh at night" he jokes then takes pity on me.

"It's okay Sarah. I appreciate your first impression. The house was built over 125 years ago by my grandfather, with the input of his father. I've been extremely fortunate to see the heritage live on. It's why I decided to quit the import business and help my father restore the Estate's finances; I want to ensure it will go on for my children and theirs someday."

I look over at him. "It's just that I never suspected it would be this beautiful. I can't wait to see the inside and no, I do not believe in ghosts." I laugh nervously.

"No ghosts, at least none that I've met; I almost wish we did have a few, I'd ask them some questions you can bet."

Bert stops the car at the front entrance then sees to my bag and the carrier while Thomas helps me from the car.

"I'll just take the bags up, Miss."

"Thank you Bert and please, call me Sarah."

"As you wish, Miss Sarah." He takes both bags into the house, setting the carrier just inside the door.

"Your domestic cat is here Miss, do you wish him upstairs or down?"

I suppress a smile, "Thank-you Bert, I'll take care of him." I steal a look at Thomas, who winks and answers, "We'll be fine, Bert."

He disappears up the front stairs as Thomas turns to me, "He doesn't appreciate the finer points of a "domestic" cat as we do I suspect."

I have to laugh, "I perceive you may be right. What shall I do with Tom? I don't want him to become disoriented and wander off, but he is used to the outdoors, at least during the day."

"I think I may have a solution, you see we have a mouser named Missy to ensure there are no "varmints" that slip by us in a house this size; there are none to my knowledge nor have I seen any since being back. I guess that says a lot for her work ethic." Thomas laughs.

"I guess it does."

"Missy has her own "quarters" shall we say, for the evenings," Thomas continues. "She returns from her daily rounds via the pet door in the kitchen and sleeps in for the night. Emily, our housekeeper, latches the pet door until morning. We could see that he's introduced to Missy, do you think they'd get along?"

"He's never been antagonistic with other cats and it sounds like a good plan; thank-you for understanding, I so appreciate this. I couldn't leave him home because my parents are in the process of moving to St Thomas.

"No problem here," Thomas replies, "I believe you'll find that with the exception of Berty, everyone else likes cats. My father rather prefers dogs, but at the moment he has none, so even he may warm up sooner or later. I'll ask John our gardener to make up another box for your room.

"Let's take a break before we grab lunch," he adds. "Come with me, I'll show you to your room so you can make sure you have everything you need."

With that he picks up Tom's carrier and leads me up the front stairs. I use the opportunity to admire the dark wood paneling of the hallway, the stairs and the thick oriental carpeting under our feet. Pictures line the stairway; some include Thomas as a young lad with his parents.

He pauses to look back as I study them and sets Tom's carrier on the top landing then comes back down to me.

"That's my mother Irene. She passed away of a heart attack when I was ten."

"She's very beautiful."

"Yes she had a beautiful soul as well. I rarely speak of her these days; it's a time I prefer not to remember." We continue up the stairs and he pauses at the top.

"This is my favorite picture of her with me and our pets." He points to a smaller picture of him with his mother and three black and white collies. They are both all smiles and one of the dogs is attempting to lick his face.

"You look happy there, so does your mother."

"We were, right up to when she left us." He walks with me down the east hallway then pauses to open the third door on the right and hold it open for me. I step into the high-ceilinged room where a beautiful chandelier hangs in its center. He flips the light switch and several lamps came to life at the bed, the desk and on the mantle of the small fireplace.

"You can turn any of these on or off as you like, but you'll need to keep the switch on if you want to control them when you enter and leave the room. The bathroom is straight through here." He points to a side door.

"Oh Thomas, it's beautiful." I exclaim and see that my bag has been placed by the closet.

"Where would you like Tom?" He asks.

"Oh my, I'd forgotten all about him. Please put him down there, I'll just let him out so that he can get used to his new surroundings." I take out a small foldable litter box from the outside pocket of my valise and place it in the bathroom. Tom steps out and takes a long stretch after his several hours of confinement then strokes around my slacks as I pet him. Thomas reaches down to let Tom smell his hand before scratching his head in the exact spot between his ears that all cats love.

"Looks like you two are instant friends." I say.

"You just have an extremely friendly feline." Thomas replies and looks up at me from the cat's side. "Ok, I'll just go downstairs to find those peanut butter and jam sandwiches." He straightens and turns to the door, "When you're ready, go out this door, turn right and continue down the hallway to the back stairs. They come down to the kitchen and there's no way you can get lost."

"Sounds simple enough; send out the constable if I'm not there in twenty minutes."

Thomas laughs, "I will do that."

I turn to look again at the room. Sort of knocks my ill expectations right out of the park along with the vision of a cramped attic room with leaky roof.

Tom jumps onto the window sill and makes himself comfortable as he gazes out the window at the yard below then begins to lick his paws and spruce up a bit.

I decide to change into something more comfortable and lay out the jeans and sweater packed in my carryon. Freshened up, I put some food and water in Tom's dish. His travels have not dulled his appetite in the slightest; he responds on the run as soon as he hears the lid snap off the can. When he begins to eat, I tiptoe out before he can follow me.

Pausing outside the door to get my bearings, I note a beautiful table and lamp sit directly opposite my door. Good landmark I think and take a right toward the back of the house as instructed. On the way, I look over the railing to see the great room below. Oh boy, I'm supposed to get used to this I think and stand in awe for a moment before continuing on to the stairs.

The back stairs lead to a nice landing halfway down where a leaded glass window looks out on the grounds behind the house. I stop to study the gardens below as a man in overalls talks to some younger men, their wheelbarrows nearby. The garden stretches to a path at its far end; what a great place for a walk I think and make a mental note to explore the grounds later.

At the bottom landing my feet come to rest on the cool stone floor of a large open kitchen. There are high cabinets lining the walls in white and several windows let in the northern light from the gardens in the back yard. Indirect lighting along the stone walls washes the granite's natural color to a soft gray. About halfway down the outside wall a huge Aga gas cooker under a hood sits and at the end of the room are several doors which I imagine may lead to cold space, pantries or facilities for this level.

At the kitchen's center is a large country table with enough seating for twenty or more, but two currently share its space, Thomas and an older woman whom I suppose might be the housekeeper from her uniform.

"Ah, here she is and no need to call out the sheriff." declares Thomas as he rises to pull out a chair for me.

"Sarah Sandlin, I would like you to meet Emily Courson, our wonderful housekeeper, the reason I stand before you today without criminal record and a university degree." he declares.

"Oh Mr. Smith sir, it wasn't as bad as all that. You were just adventuresome and you missed your mother, God bless her. I did what I could." She reached to take my hand and cover it with her own.

"My," she continues, "you look fairly starved, please sit down. Mr. Smith asked for peanut butter and blackberry-apple jam sandwiches so that's what I prepared, but if there's any room left for a nice vanilla pudding it's there in the fridge, first shelf." She points then proceeds to take off her utility apron, hanging it on a nearby hook.

"I'm off to make sure we have food for tonight's dinner. Wonderful to meet you Miss Sarah and by the way, I hear we have a new boarder by the name of Tom upstairs. Bring him down after six tonight and we'll see how he takes to Missy. See you both later." She waves and disappears through one of the doors at the end of the room.

"What an energetic woman. I wish I had half of her energy today." I tell Thomas and take a bite of the best PB and J I've ever had.

"What is this?" I ask.

"Do you like it?" Thom asks, "It's homemade peanut butter from the peanuts we grind in this kitchen. Our cook, Jamie Sellers buys them by the sack when he gets the notion to make a fresh batch."

"You've ruined me for life Thom. No longer will I be grabbing the usual factory-made jar off my market's shelf."

"What do you think of the blackberry-apple jam?" He asks.

"It's very tasty, I wouldn't have thought of combining the two, but I really do love it."

"It's Em's private recipe, she passed it on to Jamie some years past. Hope you like our home so far; do you need anything upstairs?"

"Oh my no, the room is lovely and very comfortable." I tell him and take the last bite of my sandwich.

"Would you like a tour now? I know you must be curious." Thomas asks.

"That would be wonderful, yes I can't wait." I drain the last of the cold milk in my glass.

"Good, let's go," he says, "we have a lot of ground to cover if you're to have a nap before dinner."

"How did you know?" I ask in surprise.

"I've made the trip across several times and understand how it knocks off your internal clock. A good nap will cure all, believe me. Now, you've already seen the kitchen, so let's go out to the gardens we'll come back inside through the dining room, the great room, zoom by the library then you're free to go upstairs.

"By the way, dinner is at seven right here in the kitchen and very informal. It's a family dinner, so please feel free to wear what you normally wear and are comfortable in."

He wouldn't say that I think, if he knew my usual attire for dinner is pajamas with socks.

We walk from the kitchen out to the incredibly neat rows of the garden I viewed earlier from the stairwell landing. But the late afternoon chill is beginning to settle in and I'm soon shivering in my short sleeves. Thomas takes notice and postpones our outside tour for another day.

"Shall we save this for tomorrow in view of your goose bumps?" he asks.

"I think under the circumstances my Florida skin is in shock" I laugh. He leads me to the terrace where we enter through the French doors of the dining room on the west side of the house. With the flip of a switch at the doorway, the room comes to life under its three chandeliers. A huge table and chairs anchor the length of the room.

"This table is extraordinary, I love the color of the wood; it doesn't weigh down the room."

"Thank-you,' Thomas replies, "this furniture was picked by my mother at an Estate sale; she wasn't fond of the dark wood finishes in most of the rooms and wanted this room to be especially cheerful. I think she accomplished that, don't you?"

"It's beautiful Thomas." The colors of the room remind me of a sunset; golds, tangerines, with some darker reds and blues as well.

"You'll see all her handiwork at some point during your stay with us. We have eight bedrooms and a master suite on the second floor, all with private baths and a fireplace to keep off the winter chill. There are servants' quarters and two large apartments on the third floor but currently, Emily and Margaret, our business assistant are the only residents.

"The attic on the fourth floor runs the full length of the house with a few rooms for lesser servants, all empty now. The remaining attic space acts as storage for our strange collection of furniture and antiques from various periods in the Estate's history." Thomas takes me out of the dining room as he talks.

We walk to the great room at the center of the house, its huge, mantel-pieced fireplaces at either end, with coats of arms hung over each. The room has dark oak paneling halfway up its walls to the height of the fireplace and plastered walls up to the overhang of the second floor.

Several French doors, one either side of the southern fireplace and three down the outer wall, open out to the terraces and flood the grand space with their eastern light.

"Wonderful design," I remark, "these doors really light up the room."

"Thank you," Thomas says proudly. "This room used to be a meeting hub for the area's farmers and landowners in grandfather's time. They came to discuss important issues of the day; politics, crops, roadways, transportation and such. The owners of Highbridge were host to important decisions for the community and we'd like to share a greater part in that process again."

The last stop is the library where I will do most of my work.

"All these books came here via the residents of the house, my grandfather, his father as well," Thomas explains. "Dad brought many good books to these shelves through the years. These over here," he walks to a lower shelf, "were mine when I was little." I take a closer look and see Robinson Crusoe, the Three Musketeers and many other children's classics.

"Dad had them placed low so that any child, including me, could easily reach them. He believes children should be able to help themselves to a book whenever they want."

With that, Thomas releases me from the tour; I have to admit the comfy mattress I'd earlier tested with a trial bounce now calls to me. I slowly climb the front stairs and notice someone, probably Emily, has turned on the light across the hall from my door, making the way clearly visible. Nice touch I think as I open the door to flip on the light switch.

Tom is comfortably ensconced on the bed and looks up at me from one eye to satisfy his curiosity then lays his head back down to return to whatever it is cats dream of. I take off my shoes and join him, pulling a soft throw up over me. I'll sleep an hour then take a shower.

I feel Tom's sandpaper tongue on my nose and open my eyes to see him peering at me.

"Okay, okay big boy, let's get you something to eat." I sit up and look at the clock on the mantle first which shows seven o'clock.

"Oh no," I think of dinner, "I'm late. But as I jump out of bed, I happen to look out the window. Morning sun floods over the horizon; I realise with a shock that last night's dinner is history and my tomorrow is today.

I've really blown the schedule so I slow to my usual morning pace then hear a light knock on the door. I look in the mirror over the sink and groan, let the person knocking beware.

When I open the door, I find Emily with a pot of coffee and some scones on a tray. God bless her.

"You are just what the doctor ordered Emily, how wonderful. Come in. I'm so sorry I missed my first dinner with everyone." I clear a spot on the desk for the tray.

"Oh now Miss Sarah, don't worry about that, everyone understood perfectly and we agreed we would not call or try to rouse you. How do you feel this morning?" She pours a cup for me.

"Well actually, I feel fine; guess I really needed that sleep to recover."

"Wonderful, I will report to Mr. Thomas since he asked. As it turned out, Mr. Stephen had business in London so he stayed the night. So we'll just try it again tonight when everyone is present." She smiles as she asks "Can I get you anything else?"

"No, no, you've already done much more than I deserve; thank-you Emily."

"Very well." Then she adds "Our regular breakfast time is usually 8 am in the kitchen. The men like the casual table, besides, the direct access to the back door is handier for the garage or grounds, wherever they work; I can't say I blame them. Right then, see you downstairs, don't hesitate to call me if you need anything."

After a hot cup of coffee and a scone, I feel ready for the shower I'd meant to take last night. Tom has finished his left over food and lays on the window sill watching some squirrels chase around the trees.

Much better I decide afterwards and dress in jeans with a t-shirt then throw a large, oatmeal-color cardigan over my shoulders. Looking in the mirror I see that the steam from the shower has my hair all curly. Yup, strays and ringlets; oh brother, it's grade school all over again. But no time to straighten it and be on time for breakfast, so it will have to do.

I need to ask Emily about shopping in the neighborhood for Tom's food I think as I walk down the back stairs to the kitchen to discover wonderful smells.

Thomas sits at the table with an attractive older woman, her red hair frosted with a natural silver and an older, very distinguished-looking man who must be his father Stephen.

"Good morning everyone." I say as I enter and Thomas rises to pull out a chair for me.

"All tiptop after your rest?" He asks.

"Oh yes, I feel so much better. Thank you all for understanding, please forgive me for missing dinner."

"No problem, really." He then turns to introduce his father. "Sarah, I'd like you to meet my father, Stephen."

Stephen rises to his feet to take my hand, "I've heard so much about you Sarah, splendid to meet you. May I introduce you to my longtime assistant at Smith Imports, Margaret Jenkins. Meggs, as we affectionately call her, has consented to work with us here at the Estate and now lives in her apartment on the third floor."

"How do you do Sarah, so nice to meet you" She smiles warmly at me.

"Please everyone, sit down." Stephen calls out, "Let's polish off this huge breakfast Jamie's prepared for us. Oh, you haven't met Jamie, our cook. Jamie, where are you my boy?" A blonde-haired young man of about twenty four appears from one of the doors at the end of the kitchen to answer "Yes sir?"

"Come meet our guest, Jamie." Stephen introduces me as "Sarah, who's come all the way from the U.S. to help us define our lineage and find out the family secrets."

"You must be the one who made that delicious peanut butter in my sandwich yesterday."

"Yes Miss, I did, thank-you." A little embarassed, he excuses himself to return to his chores, "Please enjoy your breakfast."

The table is laden with a server of sausage, bacon, grilled tomatoes, eggs sunny side up and toast.

"Let me just remark if I may, if you feed me like this every day, I will need to reserve two seats to my usual one to fly back to the States." Everyone laughs then passes me a hearty share of the staples which I take without protest.

We relax at the table afterwards to sip coffee while Thomas and Stephen discuss the Mill and its timetable for completion.

"The use permit from the County council and the Environmental Agency was approved this week," Stephen explains, "it went in our favor the stream runs through the middle of the Estate since, if raised to a level of three to four feet, it won't affect the neighboring farms."

"They checked the required design for the stream's course into the mill wheel as we expected." Thomas adds. "Having already included the required feature to keep fish and aquatic life out of the channel, our plans couldn't have been better presented."

I listen closely and find it interesting since I'd never been on the "inside" of a mill plan.

"Margaret, are you used to hearing all this technical talk by now?" I ask her.

"Not really, but it's far more interesting to me than commodities were in my past position. We should have lunch this week and get better acquainted Sarah; compare notes so to speak, what do you think?"

"I think it's a great idea. Put me down for Wednesday, I'll probably need a break by then. And by the way, do you know the closest place to shop for personal supplies, shampoo and the like while I'm here? I feel so helpless without a car."

"Of course." Megg answers, "See that bulletin board over there; just put your needs on the list with your initials beside. If early enough, you'll have them the same day, otherwise the next. Bert goes into the village daily, he'll pick up what you need with the regular order."

"Wonderful, thanks Megg." I do as told and also enter a week's worth of cat food to the board.

Thomas asked me earlier to meet him in the Library after lunch and he's just turning off the news as I arrive.

"Sarah, good timing. I want to show you where the materials are that you may be interested in." I follow him to the corner of the room furthest from the door where he turns on an overhead light near the bookshelves.

"These shelves contain all the ledgers I know of, pertaining to my father's father, Charles; his tax reports on this house, his church records, marriage and war records. There may be more, for I confess I haven't been able to go through the mass of info stored here."

I go to his side to glance over the various ledgers and files. It's exciting to see so much information drawn together in one place. I've never had that luxury in previous studies and it makes me eager to begin.

"This is wonderful; it could very well be the bulk of what we need to complete an initial line diagram of your family," I tell him. "I'd like to start my review this afternoon and create a catalogue of all the resources. With that done I can go forward or rather, backwards from our latest facts in search of your great grandfather."

"Of course, whatever you need will be provided; you name it." Thomas says.

"Well, just a few things," I respond. "A computer connection in this alcove, and a table or desk placed here by the shelves would greatly cut down my 'back and forth's'.

"I'll also need time with your father, perhaps an hour to start, with additional time later on. You see, most people have memories they don't realise they've retained from their childhood. I find asking them to retell stories they do remember, can lead to more. We need all the clues we can find and your father is currently the single live source we have." I write some notes to keep track of what we've discussed then continue.

"Do you have any elderly relatives or friends who might have information or experiences relating to your great grandfather?" I ask Thomas.

"I know of no one, or even if they exist, but I'll query Dad on the subject this afternoon when I see him." He answers.

"Disappointing, but perhaps we'll be able to find other completed research that links with your line, don't despair," I tell him. "You also mentioned the attic is full of old furniture and things original to this house, Thomas; have you gone through any of it for clues on your grandfather?"

"Actually, I believe the answer is "no" as strange as it sounds to me now that you ask." Thomas' face flushes a little in color.

"It's okay, we'll get through this anyway, don't worry. Now, this may sound pretty far-fetched, but are there any secret places in this house; passageways, secret drawers, or even rooms? I know you may think I've watched too much American television Thomas, but in Victorian days, certainly through wartime on this side of the world, these things were commonly built in as a way to protect art, jewelry and sometimes people. I'd like some help to conduct a thorough search of the house. We'll need to set aside at least one day to go through each room, including the basement quarters. If you have blueprints of the house, those would be useful as well."

<<>>

Sarah's plans and remarks make sense I think and I take a seat at the window to listen to her; she's very talented at this and I do admire her. If anyone can uncover the secrets of our family Sarah will and the thought pleases me.

"Do you have a question Thomas?" she sees the slight smile on my face.

"Oh, nothing except that I really am confident in your ability to get this project done," I tell her. "It all sounds spot-on Sarah and if you'll make up a calendar of events you want to schedule, give it to Meggs as soon as possible and she will coordinate them for you. I won't lie, this is a very busy time for both Dad and me, but we're on board with your research and will share as much of our time as we can."

"Thank you Thomas, I'll try not to disappoint."

"I know you won't. Now, I believe you were interested to see the Mill? I think we'd better take advantage of the weather and time while we have both, what do you think?"

"I think you're right, once I get started on this project, I'll be dedicated to it, so let's break and have some fun before I become the dusty librarian, shall we?"

I return her smile, "I can't picture you that way."

"Just you wait Thomas; I've been known to miss lunch for days in a row."

"Then I'll alert the staff to bring your lunch to the library; that solves that problem. Now go change to some wellies," I direct her, "there are extras at the back door; I'll meet you outside at the garage."

The day feels cool and crisp when I step out the kitchen door in a pair of borrowed wellies, slightly oversized but wearable. The blue sky is scattered with clouds and a flock of wild geese fly high overhead in a V-formation. The wellies crunch the gravel in the back driveway and I soon find Thomas waiting for me in the Land Rover by the garage. The Rover looks old, its color a drab olive, sort of like a military vehicle. He motions me over and opens the passenger door from the inside.

"Hop in, this is really the best way to travel down to the site, the ground is quite a mush after they cleared the site last week." I fasten my seat belt and off we go around the house out the main drive until we reach a small road. There are visible tractor tyre marks at the sides of the two-rut road and I hold to the door jamb as we bump down the hill. We finally reach the bottom pasture land then turn toward the mill site. Alongside us, the Copper Swift makes a dark cut through the property, running swift and true to its name at about forty-six metres wide, give or take. Its clear water sparkles over scattered rocks of varying browns and golds on its way downstream.

"This water joins another river further south." Thomas says as he turns off the ignition; we both push open our doors to walk around the car and watch the river.

"It has a peaceful sound don't you think?" He asks.

"It does. Are there any fish in here?"

"The salmon rarely make it up this far, but we do get brown trout for fly fishing in the spring, of course bream and smaller fish on a regular old worm. Do you fish, Sarah?"

"Why of course." I brag, "My Daddy taught me well as a kid, but it's been a long time since I picked up a worm. I've never tried fly fishing; it looks like tall people would do better than someone like me and I'm doubtful that I could master it."

"Not so. It's all in the forearm and learning how to deliver the fly like thistledown to the surface, thereby tantalising a fat trout in the process. Nothing to it; if you'd like to try, I can teach you and you can show off to your dad in the spring."

"I just may take you up on that, provided we get some time off from our schedule." I follow him along the stream to the area cleared for the new mill building.

"What will it look like?" I ask. "I've seen old mills in New England, wood construction with their wheels rotting away. There used to be one in a small town not far from where my Dad was born; unfortunately it couldn't be saved as no one had the money or interest for it."

"Wait here, I'll go to the car to get the architect's drawings." Thomas trots back to the car then returns with a copy of the artist's rendering, showing it with pride.

"This is how it will look. You see, it'll be built on a field stone foundation, gathered right here from our property which saves us money. The building itself will be three-story granite with an insulated metal roof. It will be completely vapour and heat insulated to get us through our hard winters and fully ventilated to control airborne grain dust, a huge human health and fire hazard. That precaution will save us some serious insurance money since it will be environmentally safe. These are all improvements never heard of in mills built a hundred years ago."

"What's this?" I point to an opening in the back of the building.

"That's where the water wheel shaft will enter. It's connected to several sets of gears to turn the grinding wheel faster than the rpm's of the water wheel outside which renders a smooth grind. Over here," he points to the stream on the drawing, "the water comes downstream to a dam approximately three feet higher than its present level which provides enough fall to drive the wheel. We'll use a more modern, aluminum wheel versus the old wooden type, which solves the upkeep problems."

"It all sounds very involved," I remark, "I know little about a mill's production process; the movement of the grain, what kind of flour you'll produce or who you'll sell to, but it sounds very exciting. With you and your father's combined business sense, I know you'll make it work Thom."

"Thank-you for that vote of confidence, but we are not so foolish that we think we know how to run a mill ourselves, yet." He folds the drawing, "Dad already contracted an experienced mill engineer to get us through the building stage and do production management for a period of two years. After that, he's agreed to stay on as a consultant when needed. His name is Joseph McHugh, if it weren't for his expertise, we'd be in sticky territory indeed."

We walk back to the car to climb inside. "Joe's a very active retiree from a big commercial mill in Scotland. We interviewed several applicants but are convinced he's one of the best. You'll get a chance to meet him this weekend; he'll be over for dinner on Saturday from his farm." Thomas starts the car but hesitates then turns toward me.

"It's good to have someone to talk about all this with, besides Dad. You're a good listener Sarah, you show interest with some overall understanding." Then he laughs, "I can't tell you how many of my acquaintances know less than anything about matters like this. They pretend to be interested when I talk, but do a rather bad job of it."

"Pretty transparent aren't they?"I remark. "I can identify with that. A man I briefly dated, thought genealogy applied to 'rich' people as he put it and had no idea it's actually done more these days to track family health history than for any other reason. I have no patience with that type."

We look at each other for a few seconds then turn away. Thomas puts the car in gear and we bump up the lane to the main driveway back to the garage.

We pull off our wellies at the kitchen entrance and leave them on the shelf in the breeseway to enter the kitchen. Jamie stands at the Aggie and ladles soup from a huge kettle. "How about a bowl?" He asks with a smile.

"Smells delish Jamie, thank-you. I'll just take mine to go and get busy in the library," I tell him, "I'm feeling rather guilty about the slow start on my research."

It's been a week since we arrived, Tom greets me in our room. I give him a pet with an ear rub in apology for ignoring him. He's been on prowling limitations and I try to assure him by saying, "You'll get to come downstairs to meet Missy tonight."

Emily and I decided to keep him inside the first week after all, placing his feed dish beside Missy's. I feel nervous about letting him out in a strange place, but one week should be enough to establish a new centre of the universe for him.

In the library I cross to my desk to turn on the computer, the screen immediately shows a desktop calendar page for each the house's residents. Thom's, Stephen's and mine comes up automatically along with those for the house staff. Meggs did an excellent job setting this up last week, I'm very pleased to see 'Attic Inventory' already on for day after tomorrow, following breakfast—terrific.

Everything I requested of Thomas on my first day, was in place a day later. He must have seen to it personally and I'm beginning to appreciate his sincerity about the project.

Time is flying today, a couple of hours to dinner, but these catalogue sheets will progress I declare and sit down to become quietly lost in the Estate's old tax records.

That's odd, these show Stephen's name as owner in 1976 and Charles as early as 1940 but nothing before that. I make a 'Note to self: pull up taxation laws online to see if anything changed around 1940'. I already know that at one time taxes were levied based on the number of chimneys on a house and always found that humorous, but something tells me it won't be that simple in this instance.

The grandfather clock in the hallway strikes the hour prompting me to stop work for the evening. I rise from the chair to stretch and rub my eyes after a solid two hours of work then load the heavy notebook of records back on the nearby shelf.

It's getting a little cool, I should have brought my sweater down, but as I turn from the shelf, I notice the fire across the room and realise Berty must have been in recently to light it. Nothing's changed I think, I still get lost in the work and become oblivious to my surroundings. I walk over to stand before the fire's glow and relish its warmth.

A coat of arms hangs over the mantle, different from those in the great room. There's a drape of plaid on its crossed swords; I wonder if it's part of the family's heritage, something to ask Stephen I remind myself. I turn to admire the large oak spindle table with its six chairs and the heavy wine-colored drapes now pulled shut, that would surely block the coldest of winter night air. Tall track ladders stand at each wall of shelves around the room and a paneled door leads to a half-bath. The inlaid wood parquet floor is covered sporadically with thick oriental rugs in rich colors of wine and gold. What a beautiful and cosy room this is to work in.

I've just turned off the lights to start upstairs and change for dinner when Emily crosses the great room.

"Oh Miss Sarah, I want to let you know that dinner will be a half hour late tonight. Mr. Stephen is returning from London and traffic's a little heavy on the motorway."

"Thank you Emily, I think I'll use the extra time to bring Tom down to the kitchen if you don't mind? He's been closed up in my room and could use some exercise."

"Oh my, I'm sure. Bring him down, I'll latch the pet door; Missy may already be inside, she usually smells dinner and wanders in to be underfoot. See you soon then." She walks quickly toward the front of the house to turn on the entryway lights.

Upstairs I'm greeted with a loud "meow" as Tom jumps from the bed. I bend to give him a well-deserved pet and remark "you're getting sprung tonight buddy."

I stand for a moment in front of the closet then decide on a pair of black trousers, a black shirt and an azure-blue sweater. After adding some small gold hoops to my ears and a gold ID bracelet Mom and Dad gave me last Christmas, I'm reminded of them. How happy they were the last time we saw each other. They'll be gone to St Thomas when I return and it's strange to think of them someplace else and not a short drive from my house. I'll call them tomorrow to wish them well.

I check myself in the bathroom mirror; funny how some things like straightening your hair lose importance when you're busy.

I walk to the door where Tom waits.

"Are you ready?" I gather him up in my arms to carry him to the kitchen. "If I allow you to follow me, we'd arrive downstairs sometime tomorrow as you inspect every nook and cranny between here and there."

I walk down the hall to the back staircase and arrive at the kitchen just as a large, fluffy calico cat enters via the pet door from outside. Tom hasn't missed her arrival; I feel him tense then he jumps out of my arms to the stone floor where they stand still, sizing each other up for a bit. Finally, they casually touch noses and Tom follows Missy over to a food dish and water dispenser in the corner. Well, that was easy, I think. Jamie smiles from the stove where he busily stirs a saucepan's contents.

"Good evening Miss Sarah. I see we have a new guest." He nods toward the corner of the room.

"Yes, I hope you don't mind. Emily and I talked about easing Tom into the daily routine around here and we decided tonight's the night to begin."

"No trouble, we've had the mouser Missy with us for several years, since before I arrived in fact and she'll introduce Tom to the finer points."

"What are we having for dinner Jamie?" I walk over to peer into the pan he stirs.

"Pork chops, with a little red wine sauce, braised potatoes and green beans, last of the season in the garden." He takes the sauce pan off and pours the mixture over the pork chops which are already browned and on low flame on a back burner. "Would you like something to drink Miss Sarah? We have iced tea, soft drinks?"

"I think a soft drink, cola if you have it, I can get it if you point me to it." I tell him.

"Drinks are in the cooler over there, door on the right. Thanks for your self-service, I'm a bit busy right now." He turns back to the stove, "Glasses, if you want one, are in the cupboard just over there." He motions to his right.

I successfully find a glass and navigate to the cooler then sit down at the table already set for dinner.

"So how long have you worked for the Estate, Jamie?"

"I started out of high school, well actually before. Have you seen the two lads who help John with the gardening? I used to be one of those. Mr. Smith recruits a few young men from the Village school every year to help with winterising the Estate and to open up the gardens in the spring. They also do odd jobs that John can't handle. Mr. Stephen knows all the families and their circumstances pretty well; he pays a fair wage. Anyway, I happened to mention that I enjoyed cooking to help my mam on the farm and Mr. Stephen overheard me say it. Next thing I knew, he'd gotten some brochures on a cooking school in Manchester and called me in to talk about my future."

"How did you take that?" I ask.

"Well, in amazement, actually. Who'd take an interest in a nobody like me?" He smiles, "But I knew I wouldn't get the chance every day and I'd better take advantage. Before you could count to ten, I accepted his offer and Mr.

Berty drove me back and forth to the tram station in York five days a week. I completed the school in 2010; soon my loan will be paid off with Mr. Stephen. Not bad for a Village kid, eh?"

"So Stephen held you to an indenture?"

"That's the way we worked it out, my father wouldn't have it any other way," he rolls his eyes, "but it's been good for me to get some experience cooking here for the house before striking out on my own; it was the right decision. I owe a lot to Mr. Stephen's interest in my welfare. That's a debt that will never be repaid."

"What's next?" I ask, remembering the same question from Judy.

"I dream of my own restaurant someday, small, nothing fancy, just good food, fresh ingredients right off the farm, sort of what we do right here, you know?" Jamie smiles and turns to the oven to check the potatoes.

We both pause as Thomas enters from the back door.

"Hello there." He unzips his jacket and hangs it loosely on one of the brass hooks along the wall. His face is flushed and Jamie asks "Been for a run sir?"

"Yes, down to the mill and back. It's that return trip that really gets the blood pumping, the hillside gets pretty steep toward the top of the run. How are you this fine evening?" He asks me then crosses to the sink to wash his hands and splash his face.

"I'm good. I spent a couple of hours in the library this afternoon and made some headway on the catalogue of resources there."

"Glad to hear it, quite a way to go I imagine?" Thomas finishes and joins me at the table.

"I think another eight hours should do it, but tomorrow we tackle the attic so the library will have to wait until we finish." I begin to feel the familiar pressure of my scheduled work build in my shoulders. Mom always accused me of taking work too seriously and trying to complete things too soon; she's probably right. Once started, I continue ruthlessly until the task is complete.

"Well, no rush, I want you to take what time you need and not feel you must hurry on this project. Highbridge is yours until you feel you're finished here," Thomas reassures me.

"About that," I take advantage of our time to bring up a concern of mine, "we haven't discussed how to track my time for you and I guess you've seen the calendar that Meggs created for us?"

"Yes, she's quite efficient isn't she." Thomas smiles.

"I began logging my time on paper, but I think, why not log it on the calendar so that you and Stephen can see the hours I'll be charging?" I tell him. "That way, there'll be no question in anyone's mind and it will help me to see where the days go, too."

"I like the idea Sarah, go ahead with that. Now, how about..." Stephen's entrance into the kitchen causes interruption.

"Hello everyone." he calls loudly, hanging his jacket next to Thomas's, he rubs his hands together.

"Bit of a chill out there tonight." Proceeding to the stove to investigate the evening's dinner, he breathes in the aroma then tells Jamie "Ho, you've got one of my favorites here."

"Yes sir" Jamie answers with a big smile; Stephen claps him on the back declaring "Capital." He turns to the table but in doing so, he notes the large yellow cat lying next to Missy in the corner of the kitchen.

"Good heavens, who's this? Thomas, you said a domestic, not a small tiger." He looks serious, but then laughs at the alarm on my face.

"There, there, just joking" He approaches Tom who watches his coming with interest.

"Quite the royal aren't you?" Stephen doesn't attempt to touch him though, returning to take a seat at the table. Within a few minutes we're joined by Megg.

Looking around at those seated, Stephen invites loudly, "Let's eat." Jamie brings all servers to the table family-style.

"This is lovely," Megg remarks, "I've eaten alone the last few years of my life and I so appreciate being part of this family group. I wonder if I can ever dine alone again after a few weeks of this."

I help myself to more vegetables while everyone takes turns describing their day to each other. The food begins to disappear as most take seconds to "clear up the leftovers" urged on by Jamie.

"Dessert anyone?" Jamie inquires, as we sit back from the delicious meal.

"Oh my," I declare, "I really can't." Megg and Thomas say the same. Stephen asks "What have you prepared?" We all laugh as his face grows red in embarrassment that he is the only 'glutton' in the group.

"In my own defense, I've been good all day, no sweets; I deserve a little treat." He begs. We assure him that we understand and Jamie places a piece of lemon meringue pie in front of him at that moment which makes the rest of us almost drool.

"Shall we move to the great room?" Thomas asks. "There's a wonderful fire on the grate and we can relax with our drinks. Dad, bring your pie and join us." So we push back from the table to walk upstairs via the servant's stair through the dining room.

The couches and two over-stuffed side chairs have been pushed to the north side fireplace so we can enjoy the view of the fire. The lights are soft in the room making the fire that much cosier. Small side tables and a large tea table in front of the couches provide space for our cups and Stephen's dessert plate.

"This is just wonderful." I comment. "I'm surprised how close and intimate this huge space feels; I would have imagined it rather barn-like in its size, but it's really quite nice."

Then I realise how that must have sounded and attempt to make it better; "I mean, the size is unusual for this small-town girl; why my living room alone would fit three times into this room." I look around to see myself the center of attention and stop talking, totally speechless. I've done it again and made a fool of myself over the size of this beautiful house.

"I'm sorry, you can take the girl out of the country, but you can't take the country out of the girl." Everyone begins to laugh and I say, "Please forgive me."

"You're still in the adjustment period here Sarah, doesn't surprise me at all." Thomas laughs. "I know somewhat of what you speak. I spent five years in dorm rooms the size of the small pantry in the kitchen while at university; add to that my roommate's habit of his laundry on the floor until washday. Whenever I came home on break, I had to reorient myself to the enormity of these rooms all over again."

"Thank-you for trying to save me from myself," I reply, "but I still feel guilty. I love this old house especially now that I know its residents. I want to thank all of you for making me feel so very welcome and a part of your lives here."

Stephen speaks up; "You are welcome my dear and we hope you'll remember us when you return to the States and keep in touch even after your work here is done." The others join in to add their good wishes, too.

The family's conversations from last night are still fresh on my mind this morning when I wake up. The sun peeks through a space between the draperies just enough to illuminate the chandelier over the bed, causing hundreds of little prisms to appear on the walls.

I hear a familiar "meow" at the door and smile as I tumble out of bed to open it. No need for an invitation; Tom enters followed by Missy and leads the way directly to the bathroom for his old feed dish, where both cats begin to eat in earnest.

"Okay, nice to see you as well fella and welcome to our restaurant Missy."

I begin to pull out my faithful Levi's and a sweatshirt for the day's attic adventures. Bound to be dusty up there, I may as well show them how I dress in real life.

By the time I'm dressed, Tom and Missy are giving me that "please open this door" look. I grab my laptop; both cats exit stage right down the hallway so I follow.

Jamie is in the kitchen preparing a huge breakfast and it smells great. But I've already promised myself to eat half of my usual.

"Do you have any whole-grain cereal Jamie?" I ask as I enter the kitchen. He pulls out a large, dry storage container with granola inside.

"This is made with grain right from this area, Sarah," he says and he points me to the cereal bowls. I notice the granola is naturally sweetened with honey and different from what I'm used to, but I retrieve some cold milk from the cooler and sit down to breakfast.

He brings a server of sausage to the table and I help myself. They're browned on the outside, juicy inside, just the way I like and I savor their spicy taste. Thomas and Emily join me half-way through my sensible feast and both are dressed to match me in Levi's with old shirts.

Orange sections are at the center of the table and I finish off with several bites. After a good strong cup of coffee, I feel ready to conquer any old attic.

We chit-chat a little on our way up to the third floor servant's quarters and the door at the end of the hall to the attic.

Thomas unlocks it and spreads it open to reach for the light switch. We follow the stairs to the attic and I stop at the top to survey the enormity of it. Windows on the east side let the sun in to illuminate the dusty air as it settles about draped furniture pieces. On the other side of the attic, overhead lights reveal several trunks, children's toys and further back under the eaves, what looks like stage scenery.

"Leftovers from a fund raiser my mother managed" Thom explains as he follows my line of vision.

"Ah" I slowly walk over to the draped furniture. "Shall we start with the large pieces first?"

"Right." Thomas reaches for one of the drapes over a shape in the front row.

"I'll rely on you Thom to tell me which pieces are newer and which are vintage, especially any that are original to the house, okay?"

"Got it. This dresser was bought in my lifetime so I doubt you'd be interested." He replaces the dust cover and digs further back to the eaves until he uncovers another piece.

"Over here Sarah."

I hear him call from inside the pathway he's opened up and find him with a very old, well-worn desk.

"Wow, that's beautiful."

"I seem to remember it as a boy. Here, let me move some of these pieces away so that we can get a better look."

I open and close drawers, peering inside with my flashlight. The desk looks hand crafted by a talented woodworker and I take out my cell phone to snap pictures for later scrutiny.

"Did your grandfather use it when you arrived, Thomas?"

"I don't remember it at four years of age, bear in mind he passed when I was just five. But I do remember it later as one of my favorite places to hide under when my mother and I played hide and seek."

"Well, it's impressive; original to the house or you wouldn't remember it before your mother started to bring in pieces later."

"You know, you're right...that hadn't occurred to me."

I enter the description of the desk to my laptop then move on with Thomas to continue the search. We pull off and replace several dust covers, until we come to a large chest of drawers, inset with ash veneers, almost French in its style.

"This is different than what we've seen so far."

"I don't remember this at all."

Emily joins us after finishing a sort-through of some children's dressers on the west side of the attic. "I believe it was your mother's. Your father brought it into the master suite for her, after Charles's death. The rooms were very masculine in your grandfather's day; Stephen wanted to give it a little feminine touch for her." She's smiling as she speaks of the memory.

I take a picture of the chest and add the location in the attic in case we need to find it again. We split up and continue to look through the collection. I call to my two helpers, "Don't forget to look under cushions and down the backs."

Thomas finishes the draped furniture then moves on to the old trunks which sit in the north end of the attic. Some have itemised labels, but most do not.

He chooses one that looks the oldest, pulls it out into better light and lifts two latches on the lid. Inside he finds an old WWII officer's uniform with some slight moth damage, but otherwise in good shape. He looks at the id inside the jacket.

"Sarah, Emily, come see what I've found."

When we arrive, he holds up the uniform; "It's my grandfather's." He drapes it carefully over a nearby trunk. "And look, here are his medals." We gaze in awe at several medals, each in its own presentation box.

"Here are more...wait a minute...these are much older."

"They certainly look older, maybe they belonged to his father?" I look at Thomas who returns my stare.

"I think we should take this trunk down to the library, what do you think?"

Emily suggests that Berty could bring it down as soon as possible. I take a picture of the trunk with its lid open before helping Thomas replace the uniform then close the lid securely.

"I say we deserve a break for lunch." Emily speaks up, "it's almost one o'clock." We brush off dust before walking downstairs.

Jamie directs us to the west terrace for lunch and we take a shortcut around the house from the kitchen door.

"Well, this is a scurvy bunch of adventurers, if ever I saw one." Stephen laughs and secretly observes that Miss Sarah's nose has dust on the tip, Emily's hair has gone all askew and Thomas' shirt lays wrinkled outside his belt.

"Thanks a lot Dad. We didn't see you up there uncovering years of dust and grime."

"Oh that's not in my schedule for today, or any other day frankly. I'd much rather sit here with a good paper and wait for the full report."

We all give good-natured laughs and sit down to load up our plates with sandwiches, potato crisps and fresh-picked salad. The afternoon has been fairly sunny but clouds begin to gather on the horizon; Stephen mentions the weather report calls for rain this afternoon.

"In that case, we probably should wind this up. It's already dark up there, it'll be worse when the rain begins. We can always schedule another day to finish up if need be. Emily, after lunch could you ask Berty to bring that trunk to the library today?"

"What trunk?" Stephen responds to the word.

"We believe one could have belonged to your father, it's full of war medals and uniforms. There are also some older medals that may have been from before his time. You'll have to take a look to see if you recognize them."

"Sounds intriguing; let me know when the trunk is down and we'll go through it together." He rises from his chair.

"I'm off to the Grange to talk with Jack Andrews about his recommendations for our farm manager position."

Dad's intent to take initiative for the farm rather surprises me, but since I've been tied up with the Mill's construction, it is a relief of sorts.

"Sounds like a good idea, I'd planned on visiting Jack myself but if you're willing, we can discuss the visit at tomorrow's meeting?" He agrees and waves goodbye to all as he heads for the garage.

"He hasn't slowed down in the slightest has he?" Megg observes as she joins us.

"No, and I don't expect he will anytime soon," Thomas remarks. "The difference is that he's doing what he likes for a change and that makes it fun, not work."

He and I finish up our lunch then take bottled water back to the attic with us. Emily appeared a little tired from the morning's forage and had duties around the house this afternoon so we excused her. She protested, but gave in.

"Alright, where were we?" Thomas asks.

"I believe we left off over here," I walk along the west aisle of the attic, "with the trunks." I stare at the twenty or more trunks under the eaves feeling a little daunted.

"Let's start with this one and we'll make short work of them before teatime, what do you say?" Thomas suggests.

Must he be so cheerful I think, but then realise I am looking forward to the excitement of the search.

"Sounds like a plan."

We open, examine then close ten of the twenty trunks; five contain clothes of Thom's mother, including formal wear from parties she and Stephen hosted.

The other five contain some of Stephen's clothes from his years as a svelte young man when his midsection paunch hadn't developed.

We stop for a break and sit on the floor, drinking from our water bottles.

"How do you feel, as you see this old memorabilia Thom?"

"Rather nice to remember things forgotten about my Mother. Seeing her dresses brings back some happy times and makes her seem close. Didn't I hear you say your parents were moving to St. Thomas?"

"They're so excited to pursue their dream; actually Dad invested my unused college fund to make it possible. Can you imagine? My father invested in social media at its startup. It's just a hoot for me to see them able to take this adventurous move of theirs."

"You love them very much." Thomas says.

"We're close; they were there for me after Brian's death, though I failed to return their attention for several years."

"I remember Brian in school," Thomas tells me. "He was always talking about his beautiful wife at home, missing you and so hopelessly in love."

"I missed him, too. The nightmare of losing him forever was almost more than I could bear. I couldn't move on with my life." I stop to look at Thomas.

"You and your father are partly responsible for finally pulling me out of that." I say to him.

"What do you mean?" Thomas asks.

"You wrote to me and invited me here. I didn't even remember you Thom, but the thought of a chance to do something new gave me the push to step forward. Here I am, doing what I love, in a beautiful new place, with good people all around. Thank you for that."

He blushes at my little speech and jokes, "You didn't remember me. That good looking friend of Brian's that you met while on vacation. How could you forget me? I'm hurt." He laughs and makes an effort to stand up.

I pull him back by the arm saying, "No, you don't understand. I was so young, so in love—it could have been the King of England and I would have forgotten him with Brian in the room."

"Well, that puts me in some pretty good company, so I guess I don't feel quite as bad." Thomas says with faux timidity.

"If it's any comfort," I tell him, "after we talked and I accepted your offer, I remembered your voice and your laugh over Tom's meowing. I felt like a complete idiot for not recognising you as one of Brian's best friends."

"We had a funny way of proving that didn't we?" Thomas says. "Both of us so busy after school, we hardly kept in touch. That's when I married Lydia."

"You mentioned her in your letter to me. I thought it rather odd to use an ex-wife for a character reference." I can't help throwing a raised eyebrow at him.

"Yes, I suppose it is to some, okay to most people," Thomas says, "but Lydia is different. We've known each other since childhood, went to the same schools; our parents knew each other from the time we moved here, hers still live across the fields at Roseview farm. Lydia and I were buddies through the teen years and shared a lot of teenage angst with each other." He can't help but roll his eyes then continues.

"One day after we graduated from university, we thought, 'we're such good friends, shouldn't we get married' and we did. But after a year of it, we figured out our mistake and unilaterally agreed to break it to our parents. We parted, had it annulled, but remain friends to this day."

"Just like that?" I ask him.

"Just like that." He replies.

"Where is she now?"

"London. She has her own boutique, designs that trendy clothing stuff that tourists just eat up and sells it all over the world on the internet, too. She's very happy in her life, I'm happy for her. Marriage ruined our relationship and we realised it then moved on—end of story."

"Ok, now the character reference makes sense." I tell him. He stands up and extends his hand to help me up but can't seem to let go for a few seconds.

"We really need to finish the rest of these trunks." I say and turn away to get to work." Thomas stands quietly for a few seconds after I continue down the line of trunks again.

"Thomas, have you ever seen this mark before? It looks familiar, but I can't place it."

He comes to bend over the trunk and notices an indentation on its side; an engraved mark, similar to a shell of some sort.

"No, I've never seen it before, but it looks like a mariner's mark. Sailors used to place a mark on their trunks to identify them."

"That's interesting." I stand back to look at something else.

"Look at the size of this trunk compared to the others; it's much larger, sturdier. Did you have any ancestors who were sailors?" I ask him.

"Not to my knowledge, but Dad may know. Perhaps we should have Berty bring this trunk down as well?" We move the trunk over to the attic door with the first one.

At that moment a crack of lightning close by makes us both jump and we agree that being in the attic right now isn't such a good idea. We reach the bottom of the attic stairs as another roll of thunder announces itself and rain begins to pelt the roof.

"Well, I guess we've been lucky to have a few sunny days. At least you received a bright welcome Sarah, but I'm afraid you'll see what it's really like to live in the U.K. now." He laughs as we walk down the hall to take the stairs.

"It's ok. I'm used to the summer weather in the south back home. Every day around four it clouds up and rains with lots of wind and lightning for a couple of hours. You should see what it does for my garden though; it looks like a rain forest, everything grows so well."

"Yes, but the problem here is that it can stay cloudy and overcast for days and it isn't summer. If you're a person who loves the sun, you may start to feel light-deprived after a couple of weeks." Thomas warns and we continue down to the kitchen.

"Do you? Stay light-deprived I mean"

"Yes, I have to admit, at times I do and I've lived here all my life."

"There you both are," Emily calls from the other side of the kitchen as we walk in, "We were ready to send in a search party for you."

"Safe and sound Em," Thomas answers, "we left the attic when the lightning started."

Emily walks over to watch the rain with us through the back door. "A downpour," she notes as the driveway begins to puddle up.

"How about some tea?" she suggests. "I'll just brew up some up for us. Jamie's left us some nice sandwiches and little cakes, too."

"Sounds wonderful Em, but I'm going to run upstairs to change out of these dust-covered clothes first, be right back," and Thomas ducks up the stairs.

"I'll do the same Em, be back in a few minutes." When I reach my room, I remember my promise to call Mom and Dad and check the time; better do it now I decide and dial their number on the land line.

"Hello, Sarah?"

"Yes Mom, who else would be calling you from the U.K.? How are you; how are the moving plans going?"

"Oh it's so good to hear your voice dear and the move is going great. In fact we're ahead of schedule; we've already shipped what furniture we basically need for our condo. You know it's hard to buy furniture once there and expensive."

"Yes, I've heard that. How's Dad with all this?"

"He's persevering quite well actually and can't wait to take up the life of a beachcomber." Mom laughs, "Would you like to say hello?"

"Please."

"Hello daughter, how's the U.K.?" I hear Dad on the other line, "Soaking up that rainy weather?"

"Actually, it just rained for the first time today and it is a soaker. I hear you're ahead of schedule on the move?"

"We are," He answers, "You know what a great organizer your Mom is. It looks like we may already be moved by the time you get back Stateside."

"I'm sort of prepared for that actually, since I'm not sure just when I'll return yet. Things are going well, but it's taken more time than I thought it would. We just finished a hunt through the attic for clues to their grandfather and I'm standing here dusty from head to foot."

"Then you must be happy as a pig in mud. I know you well." Dad laughs.

"Yes you do; listen, I'm due at tea downstairs and I need to clean up a little. Give my love to Mom, you two take care; I'll send some pictures on your cell phones soon."

"Ok dear, love you."

"Love you both, bye."

I quickly strip off my dusty clothes and throw on a clean pair of sweat pants with a long-sleeved cotton sweater, wash my face and hands then hurry back down to tea feeling somewhat human again,.

When I enter, Thomas, Emily, Megg and Stephen are already at the table.

"Here she is." Stephen gets up to pull out a chair for me.

"Sorry everyone, I decided to call home and touch base with Mom and Dad"

"That's good" Megg smiles, "how are they?"

"They're fine. Their moving day may be sooner than planned, they've already shipped furniture to St Thomas."

"Sarah's parents are moving lock, stock and barrel to the island to spend their retirement years. Isn't that wonderful?" Thomas explains.

"Oh my, will you be visiting them in that beautiful place, too?" Meggs inquires.

"Yes, they made sure the new place has a guest bedroom for visitors, so I'm all set."

"Well, with this weather, the islands sound like heaven." Emily says. "Your grandfather had ties in St Thomas, did you know that Mr. Stephen?"

"Yes, a distant aunt or uncle of his lived there, back when it was an island covered with coconuts, but that's all I know," Stephen says after a sip of tea. "Charles

111

mentioned it once, but didn't elaborate. At the time, I was in my twenties and my interests were on anything but dusty relatives." Stephen laughs as he takes a bite of his sandwich.

"You see; this is why we need to talk," I tell them, "sometimes there's information hidden in people's minds that can be useful." My enthusiasm just doubled, "You and I have an appointment to talk Stephen and we'll do just that."

"Now don't get your hopes up Sarah girl, you may be surprised to learn just how little I or even my father knew about the family history. Some people live in the present and don't bother to think of those in the past."

"Understood and please don't think I'm faulting you; I enjoy a good search and you're slated tomorrow to help me, so be prepared."

"Is she this hard on you my boy?" He asks Thomas.

"Dad, you should have seen her dig through the attic. Do you know how much we've shoved up there over the years? Sarah is a dynamo, thank heaven the lightning started and gave me an excuse to quit." Thomas shoots a smile at me that I can't interpret.

Chapter 5 Rain 1-2-3

The rain continues this morning, although a little lighter than through the night. I gaze out the window at the gray clouds over the forest and see a young red fox dart into the woods. Three crows sit on the fence throwing their heads back to call their loud raucous words. Below in the yard, John walks around the house toward the gardens in his wellies and yellow slicker. Surely he doesn't garden in this weather. But he keeps up a good pace around the corner of the house and disappears from sight.

A chill came on the house last night but the electric room heater certainly did the trick to make it very snug in here. I told Berty earlier not to bother with laying a fire in my room as I won't be upstairs that long this morning. My room...it hasn't taken long for me to think of it in that way.

I follow the thick wool carpet to the bathroom's pink granite floor and a hot shower before breakfast. The huge footed tub at the other end of the room reminds me how much Mom loves a good soak; she'd totally enjoy this tub, guess I miss her already.

After my shower I wrap up in one of the warm towels from the heated rack to dry my hair then dress in my usual sweat pants, shirt and sweater.

In short order I'm on my way down the hall to breakfast, but glance over the railing to see Tom and Missy walking around sofas and fireplaces, sniffing for any unfortunate types that might be in their territory. Laughing at the sight, I realise Tom is in training to be a mouser. I must tell Mom and Dad on our next check-in.

Jamie has a large breakfast ready, but hot oatmeal off the stove and a sausage or two are what I need. Butter and brown sugar on the oatmeal, cream and a spoonful of sugar to my coffee and...wow, that rain is really noisy. I walk to the window to watch rivulets down the glass while I stir my coffee. Calmed and quieted by the rain, almost hypnotized, I stare into it.

"Good morning" Thomas enters in his usual cheery way and startles me back to reality.

« »

"Oh Sarah--I'm so sorry." She jumps and coffee spills over the side of her cup.

"I didn't mean to startle you," I tell her. "Here, let me get a towel." I grab one from the counter and return to help, relieved when I find just a little on her sleeve and most of the spillage on the floor.

"I need to curb my cheerfulness in the morning" I joke as I mop up the floor, "I tend to get overly boisterous for most people at this hour."

"No, it's ok, no damage done," she laughs, "please don't stop being cheerful on my account. It's rather nice to see a morning person. You see, I've always been a night person; when I wake up, it takes me a little while to get up to speed."

"Ah, I will remember that in future." I tell her as we experience that stare between us again, when the world seems to drop away and everything goes silent.

"I have some oatmeal over here cooling, would you like some?" she invites.

"Yes that sounds good, but don't bother, I'll get it." I tell her.

"No bother, sit down Thomas, I'll bring it." She fills a bowl to put in front of me, along with a cup of tea.

"Thank you very much. You seem to have learned your way around the kitchen, Sarah."

"Yes, Jamie gave me a mini-tour on dishes, the fridge and storage locations before dinner last night. He gets busy and I feel guilty asking him where everything is, so I begged for enlightenment. He's such a nice person; he told me about your father and what Stephen's done for him."

I swallow a spoonful of oatmeal before answering; "Yes, Dad's always been involved in the local economy.

He's concerned about the younger generations who leave instead of working here where they grew up. It's a lot to ask of kids nowadays, a few, like Jamie, think the same way as Dad and me. They realise that what they have here is a little piece of heaven on their own doorsteps."

"I like that, tell me more Thom."

"Dad started a sort of scholarship, if you will, for those who dream of more education. One of the young men who works with John this year, Cole Pearson, wants to become a mechanic and open a shop in the Village. If he continues to show a good work ethic here and proves he's serious, he'll be the next recipient Dad picks."

"That's wonderful, how proud you must be." Sarah says.

"I am and I want to help carry it on, that's why this Mill means so much to me. It'll give some of the locals a place to work; it may even draw visitors to the area. Who knows, it may spawn more new enterprise. Those are my goals and I'll do my best to push through with them."

"I admire your attitude and have a feeling you'll be very successful at whatever you pursue," Sarah says. "I wish you all the luck."

"Thanks, I appreciate that." The stare between us takes over again until she looks down at her watch, "Oh my, I've got to get busy, your father comes in at ten this morning for a chat."

"I'm due down at the mill as well," I reply, "Have a great day Sarah, see you at dinner?"

"Yes, you will," She smiles.

A lovely smile, I think.

I'm surprised to see Berty in the library and he's brought both trunks from the attic and placed them by the windows. There's also a nice fire on the hearth to take off the chill in the room.

"Thank you Berty for getting these down so quickly."

"You're welcome Miss Sarah. Is there anything else I can assist with?"

"No Berty, that's all."

I bring a straight chair over to the last trunk with the 'mariner's mark' to look more closely at it but find no other marks. I'll wait to open it until Stephen arrives.

Why does the mark look so familiar I wonder and look once more then remember I sent a picture to my email. Maybe I can find out more by posting it to a history blog. But Stephen arrives on time so it will have to wait.

"Good morning Stephen," I call and he focuses on me by the window.

"Good day to you Sarah, ready for our little conference?" He notices the trunks and detours to them. "Are these what you spoke of last night?"

"Yes, both of them are of interest." I walk over to show him the contents of the first trunk. "Pull that chair up and we'll go through them." I suggest and open the lid but he peers over my shoulder, too excited to sit down.

"I think this must be my father's uniform," he say, "I remember the buttons as a child and these were his medals." He picks up three boxes and opens them. "He used to tell me the enlisted men called them the Pip, Squeak and Wilfred medals." He laughs remembering his father in younger days then remembers something else.

"My father Charles never talked about his part in WWII but when he came home, he'd changed to a quieter, more reserved man than the one I knew before."

"Look at these medals; do you remember them?" I ask and put two more boxes in his hands. He finally sits down to look at their contents.

"No, I've never seen these before. I don't believe they belonged to my father, they look much older don't they?"

"Yes, Thomas and I thought that, too. I can look them up later on the internet to at least identify what campaigns they're from. We haven't looked at the rest of the things in here." I pull out some letters tied up in string from the bottom of the trunk, "What are these?" Stephen takes the packet and pulls the string off then unfolds one of the letters.

"It's a letter from my father to my mother." He looks up at me.

"I don't know if you're aware, but my mother died at an early age, much like my wife. Her death left me on my own with a housekeeper, not the nicest woman in the world, very strict and straight-laced." He is visibly moved, but continues.

"I'd like to take these to read at another time if I may and discuss their contents with you after I've read them."

"Of course Stephen, those are your letters and it shouldn't be any other way. Just please let me know if there is anything about your grandfather that would help us, okay?" He answers with a nod and puts the letters into his jacket pocket.

"So, it looks like that's all in this trunk." I replace its contents with care. "Let's take a look at this one." We move our chairs closer to the trunk with the mariner's mark.

"Do you see this?" I ask him, pointing to the mark. "Thomas said it looks like a mariner's mark, a sort of identification of the trunk by its owner. Does it mean anything to you or do you remember something from your childhood about the mark or the trunk?"

Stephen turns his full attention to the trunk. "It looks like some sort of shell doesn't it? Offhand, I don't recall any contact with this mark or the trunk."

"Let's open it." I suggest and flip the heavy catches on the lid. Stephen pulls the lid upward laying it against the wall and when we peer inside, he reaches to pick up something. It's a gold watch chain with a scallop shell fob shaped the same as the mariner's mark.

"Well, what do you make of this?" He asks and hands it to me. "I do remember this now as it hung from father's vest pocket."

I weigh the chain in my hand and ask "Did he ever tell you a story about it?"

"Not that I can think of." He takes the fob and chain back, depositing both in his pocket then returns to the trunk.

"Sorry, that seems to be my standard reply doesn't it. I don't see anything else in here that rings a bell for me. These old shirts, riding boots and hunt jacket were dad's as well but nothing special attached to them." We return all contents back to the chest and close the lid.

"Well, it's good you found some surprises," I remark. "I'll be interested to hear what you find in the letters. Any information from your father's childhood, mention of his father and mother, could serve as a beginning query for a records or online search." Then I bring up a new subject.

"We looked at this desk yesterday, do you remember it?" I show him my camera picture.

"Why yes, it was here when I and my parents arrived. After grandfather died, my father used it for many years. It's rather large and more than I needed, so I exchanged it for something smaller, my present desk upstairs in the master suite."

"Do you have any idea where the desk originated; could it be from Charles's father's Estate?"

"Well, once again, I apologize that I know very little about the desk. You know we have an excellent antique dealer in the Village, I wonder if he could take a look at it and give us some sort of date or information on it?"

"I think that's a very good idea; if you give me his contact information, I'll call him tomorrow."

Stephen writes the number for a Mr. Peyton at his shop, "Just call Berty in the morning and have him drive you over there when you're ready."

"I know we're over our hour of time," I check my watch as I say, "but before you run away, could you just tell me your earliest memory of your father, where and what it is?"

He thought for a moment then said, "That's easy; it was when I first learned to ride a horse, out back where the garden is now; must have been about five years old. Father brought home a beautiful mare, bought her from one of the farmers in the area whose children had outgrown her. He came and fetched me from the house, said he had something to show me."

Stephen stands up to stretch then continues. "He led me out into the courtyard and there she was, all saddled and ready to go and me, scared to death, hiding behind him when the stable hand brought her up to me." he laughs at the memory.

"I thought my father would be angry, he was a big man and very strict, as were most in those days."

"And was he?" I asked, caught up in the story.

"No he wasn't, I was surprised after all the trouble he'd gone to. He bent down to my level and put his arm around me until I stopped shaking. The stableman brought the reins to him and Dad pulled her head down to us. He started to pet her nose and then took my hand and we petted her together. I remember the softness of that horse's nose on my hand; it was the first large animal I'd ever touched."

"Did you ride her that day after all?"

"No, not that day, father said there would be other days and I could ride when I felt ready—smart man he was, he made me responsible for feeding her every day. It didn't take me long to wonder what it would be like to be up there on her back and I think it must have been just a few weeks when I asked father to 'help me ride her.'

"We rode together at first with me on his lap and then one day he climbed down, shortened the stirrups and let me go it alone within the barn yard fence. After that, there was no stopping me." He turns to look at me.

"Thank-you for that question Sarah, I hadn't thought of that in years."

"I enjoyed it too Stephen. Just one more request, you must have had some contact with relatives, could you please make me a list of anyone you remember, whether you know names or not? Descriptions can sometimes help too, how they dressed, what they did, where they lived, that sort of thing, anything at all."

"I'll do my best Sarah girl," he smiles, "but honestly, I have no memories of relatives here when I was older, not even connected to St Thomas as Emily mentioned. Let me think on it and I'll give you anything I come up with. Now, I really must get on with my day. Keep me up to date as you get further into this and please don't hesitate to ask me anything, though I don't seem to be adding too much to this, do I." He says in apology.

"Thank you Stephen, have a good morning." I tell him and he leaves for the mill office.

The rain continues, predicted for the rest of the week. I need a walk and decide to have a walk inside. Why not, there's enough space to do so. Besides, I haven't taken the time to study the portraits and pictures around the house and all the lovely furniture and art pieces Thomas' mother brought in.

The aroma of soup simmering on the stove downstairs smells wonderful and checking my watch, I change my mind. Think I'll postpone the walk until after lunch.

"Aha, it's the soup bandit" Thomas says as he comes through the back door, "and I've caught her red-handed!" I stick out my tongue and he laughs as he takes off his slicker and shrugs into some loafers.

"Just for that, you get no soup today Sir," I tease him. "You'll have to dish up your own as I am busy." Feigning snobbery, I sit down with my bowl and spoon.

"Well then, I guess you'll get none of this great crusty bread and butter to eat with your soup." He matches me in snobbery as he pulls the loaf from the oven where it stays warm.

"Oh not fair," I protest and look pitiful so he'll bring the bread to the table. He cuts a large piece and passes the butter.

"Thank you, sir," I say humbly. It's a potato and leek soup I discover, after sprinkling on some parmesan and taking my first spoonful.

"How does Jamie know just what to fix us for lunch?" I ask, "This is perfect for a rainy day." I pop a large bite of the bread into my mouth, followed by an "mmm-good."

"He is remarkable that way isn't he?" Thomas says. "In all fairness, I do think he picks up suggestions from everyone; Emily, Dad and Megg included, so don't hold back if you're craving some sort of wild American food you're missing."

"Hmm, I could go for a veggie pizza or a good old hamburger with lettuce, cheese, onion and tomato."

"Tell you what, let's have a night for each of us next week to request whatever it is we'd like," Thomas suggests. "We'll submit a list and Jamie can make up the grocer's list to accommodate our requests, it'll be fun."

"I love that idea." Margaret says, overhearing his suggestion on the way in. "I've been craving some steak and kidney pie, how about it?"

By this time Emily and Stephen join in with their suggestions as well.

"So it's settled for next week and we'll have a vote on the favourite." Everyone agrees there should be a small award for the most favored food. Stephen volunteers to supply the prize and we all laugh as he suggests "Perhaps a bottle of seltzer."

I begin my walk after lunch with the dining room my first stop and enter by the servant's stair from the kitchen.

The windows cast a dim light on this rainy day, but if I want to view the various pictures on the opposite walls, I'll need more light. I flip the light switch and the beautiful chandeliers over the table come alive, sparkling brightly; I take time to admire them before walking about the room. There's a painting of Stephen and Irene who look to be in their mid-twenties; she wears a blue dress with white lace trim and Stephen looks dapper in a dark suit and bow tie.

A Venetian glass mirror hangs centered on the long wall of the room, with another portrait on its opposite side. The couple might be Stephen's parents when they were young, if so, Charles appears to have been very tall as he stands by his wife's side. I look closer at something which catches my eye on Charles' waistcoat and realise where I've seen the watch fob before. As Stephen said earlier, it hung from Charles's watch chain and here it is in this portrait. I must have seen it before when Thomas gave me the abbreviated tour. I make a mental note to call it to his attention later.

Stephen's mother Alicia appears elegant and attractively thin sitting by Charles' side. She was dressed in a dark red, floor-length gown with boning at the bodice and long sleeves which came to points over her wrists. A single small pearl dangled under each ear, with a pearl brooch at her collar's neckline; beautiful I think to myself.

Collections of cut-glass pieces are displayed around the room; several are pedestal fruit bowls, beautiful serving trays and large water pitchers with glasses to match; all purposely placed where the late afternoon sun will reach their sparkle. Irene's influence can be seen as the colors of the two paintings are infused throughout the room, even to the dark red of Alicia's dress brought to the upholstery of the dining chairs and the thick, Oriental rug in its deep blues.

All in all, a beautiful room tastefully decorated. I move to turn off the lights and run directly into Thomas as he enters the doorway.

"Again, we're doing this; I'm so sorry Sarah. Are you alright?" he asks as he steadies me by both arms.

"Yes, of course, no damage," I tell him in good humor. "We seem to be blundering into each other rather often. Perhaps we need radar sensors or something."

"I guess so. What are you doing up here?" He asks.

"I decided to tour your home and combine exercise with curiosity, since I can't walk outside with all the rain. And besides, I've wanted to take some time to look at all the pictures and lovely things your mother brought into the house."

"Do you need someone to answer questions? If you do, I'm free this afternoon now that the rain has put a hold on the mill."

"Well, yes, that would be wonderful and in that case, follow me sir." I lead him to the older portrait and ask "Is this Charles and his wife?"

"Yes, that's Alicia, I'm afraid I don't know her maiden name as I wasn't born yet when she died, a few years later after this portrait was made I understand; scarlet fever."

"You and your father share that sorrow in both your lives don't you." I remark to Thomas.

"Yes, you are very lucky to have both your parents still with you, but I'm sure you know that." He tells me.

"I appreciate them every day. You don't know this yet, but earlier with Stephen, we unpacked and examined the two trunks we found in the attic. In the one with the mariner's mark, we found a gold watch fob."

"Wonderful." Thomas replies.

"Would you like to see it?" I point to it on Charles' watch chain in the portrait.

"I'll be, nice one Sarah. Do you know in all my years with this portrait, I've never taken a close look at Grandfather's watch chain? That's why it takes an objective eye to catch these things."

"Thomas, the fob is the same shape as the mariner's mark on the trunk. What do you make of that?"

"I can't imagine; strange isn't it and becoming quite the mystery," he declares and continues to gaze at the portrait.

"Well, shall we go to the great room to finish this walk? I ask him. "I'd love to explore there."

"Lead on m'lady." He flips the light switch off as we walk into the main hall.

"Now tell me what you remember about this room as you grew up." I say as we enter the great room and I take in its enormity.

"Apparently, it was quite busy in my grandparent's day," Thomas explains. "I'm told that grandmother had groups of women in from the village regularly to play bridge and also to plan charity events; dinner dances, recitals, plays, that sort of thing. She played piano quite well Dad has always said and they hosted holiday dinners for all the village families, too.

We walk slowly about the room as he continues. "Grandfather met monthly with Grange members, the local water council and farmers from the area to discuss plans for spring planting, that sort of thing. They respected his knowledge of the European trade market and he shared information gathered from his import business with them. It was a forum of sorts and anyone from the local area was welcome.

"I remember little of that taking place after we moved here and Grandfather died. Dad had the import business by then, the world was changing and he had less time at the Estate after Mother died." Thomas goes a little quiet for a moment then lights up.

"As a lonely kid I sometimes pretended there was a grand social taking place and with Dad's permission, I put this thing into use."

He hurries to the side of the room to show me a gramophone then reaches underneath to pull out a large record album, one of several stored there. After reading its label, he lays a record on the player and lays the needle gently to it.

A waltz; I laugh at the sound of it.

Thomas turns to me and bows in mock solemnity, "May I have this dance?" He extends his hand.

I knew my lack of participation in those dance classes Mom insisted I take would get me in trouble someday and now the day is here. I panic and take a step back.

He immediately drops his hand, "It can't be as bad as all that."

"Oh yes it can, Thomas. I hope you've worn your steel-toed boots."

"Nope, just my loafers," he says good-naturedly. "Now come over here and humor me." He takes my hand and gently centers his other on my back.

"Remember, one two three, one two three." Off we go and the first two steps are more like one two ouch. But after a couple of those, I start to relax and let him lead me around the room. By the end of the song, we've waltzed the entire perimeter and are smiling at each other as the music finishes. We hear clapping and cheering from the rail above and see Margaret and Stephen, calling "Bravo - Bravo" at the top of their lungs.

"Now that's the way it's done," Stephen says. "Can you run that record again if we come down?"

Thom answers "Of course I can." I groan, knowing I'll have to go around again.

"We'll be right down." Stephen grabs Megg by the hand to bring her along.

Thomas restarts the waltz; Stephen and Megg arrive and we all waltz around the perimeter of the room until the song ends. The men bow to Megg and I, which starts both of us laughing. Then they are unable to keep their composure either and just at that moment, Berty shows up from the hallway.

"Excuse me, Miss Sarah, there's a Mr. Peyton on the telephone for you. Shall I tell him you are otherwise occupied?" His eyebrows are elevated and we all stand rather awkwardly until I finally speak up.

"I'll be right there Berty, thank-you."

« »

Sarah walks quickly away from me to the phone in the hallway, but at the last minute turns to make a funny face at our little group, which starts us all off again.

After she leaves, we get ourselves back to normal and Stephen and Meggs return to work. I lag behind because I realise something surprising has just occurred. Unlikely as it may be, I think that I may be falling for this American woman.

"Thomas, are you joining us?" Dad calls to me.

"Yes, of course." I walk to Megg's desk, but my mind is otherwise occupied.

« »

"Hello, Miss Sandlin?"

"Yes"

"This is Ted Peyton from Village Antiques, how are you today?"

"I'm fine, thank-you."

"Splendid. Stephen Smith called my father yesterday and said you have some items you wish to discover the provenance of."

"Oh yes, I didn't know he'd called. Shall I bring along the photos I've taken?"

"Well, actually I would rather come see the real thing, if that's an option."

"That would be wonderful, Ted. When can you come round?"

"How about first thing in the morning, say about nine?" He asks.

"Perfect, see you then and thank-you so much."

When I return to the great room, I see our dance time has passed and I actually feel a little disappointed. Stephen and Margaret have gone about their day but Thomas remains.

"Everything ok?" He asks.

"Yes, yes of course," and I tell him about the call.

"That's great, hope Ted can give you some info. I want to take you down to the Village as soon as this blasted rain lets up. You must be getting 'cabin fever' after two weeks of our company." Thomas says.

"Well, you won't be offended will you? I am ready to see more of the countryside. I won't say I have the fever exactly, but if this afternoon is any indication, I'd say we're all under the weather." I can't help but laugh.

Thomas joins in, "I won't admit to anything, but you're very perceptive." And leaving it at that, his smile still lingers.

I return to the library to spend the rest of the afternoon searching online for anything regarding the shell imprint's connection to Thomas' family.

This morning I awake with a start to hear Tom's meow at my door then remember I have an early appointment.

"Thank-you Mr. alarm-clock," I say to my orange tiger who wanders in and rubs across my leg enroute to his food dish.

"You know you have two food dishes don't you? And I'll bet you eat from both judging by your girth these days."

I pass up the usual jeans for a pair of dress trousers, a black sweater and a colorful scarf; might as well make a good impression for Mr. Peyton on behalf of all Yanks. Tom is at his post on the windowsill as I leave my room for a quick breakfast.

Afterwards in the library, I check the computer for emails and read answers to my inquiries on the scallop shell. Nothing seems immediately pertinent; various natives of North and South America have used them as symbols of the moon, as money and as ornaments. Generally the shell is a symbol of resurrection and baptism to Christians. I sit back to contemplate how any of these could connect to Thomas's family history when Berty knocks at the doorway.

"Miss Sarah, a Mr. Peyton is here to see you, shall I bring him in?"

"Yes, thank-you Berty."

He's much younger than I expected and around my age. "Mr. Peyton so nice of you to come out here."

"No problem, my father Theo actually spoke with Stephen but he's developed a cold and asked if I would come. Please, call me Ted."

"If you'll call me Sarah. Here are the two trunks," I lead him over to the older one and point out the mariner's mark.

"What do you make of this?"

He takes a closer look then pulls out a small magnifier with a built-in light.

"It's been carved into the wood and looks original to the age of the trunk's finish. The general style of the trunk is from the early 1800's, although it is a bit sturdier than I'm used to seeing. You'll notice there are extra oak bindings at the bottom and sides that the other trunk doesn't have. I've seen these used in land transport as well as by maritime officers. As to the shell carving itself, I can't say that I've ever seen it before, but there doesn't seem to be anything unusual about it; probably meant something to the owner. Do you know the trunk's origin?"

"We suspect it may have belonged to one of Stephen's family, perhaps his grandfather. He remembered the fob of the same design from his father's watch when we found it in this trunk. Unfortunately Stephen took it with him and I can't show it to you, but it is seen in the portrait of

Charles and his wife, which hangs in the dining room. We also have these." I pull the medals from the trunk.

"These three belonged to Stephen's father Charles, but these two are unknown to him, can you tell me anything about them?" He lays the medals on top of a nearby table and recognizes the ribbon color of one as an India General Service Medal, probably issued in the early 1900's.

"The other, I think, may have been issued in New Zealand during the land wars, but I will reserve judgment until I can research them both further. He takes pictures then replaces them in their respective boxes.

"Considering their age, they're in fair shape on their fronts, but do have very heavy wear on their backs and edges; apparently not always kept in their boxes through the years. I'm not an expert on these Sarah and I'll have to do some digging, or consult with someone more knowledgeable."

"That's fine Ted, I appreciate that. We also found a desk upstairs you might be interested in, if you're not afraid of getting a little dusty?"

"Dust is a risk of my business; let's have a look at it." He replies with a smile.

I turn on the overhead lights in the attic and lead him to the desk at the back of the space. He squeezes through the narrow access while I wait in the aisle. Time passes and I become curious when he doesn't say anything.

"What do you think?" I finally call to him.

"It's quite old and the workmanship is beautiful. I have no idea what the wood is at this point, very unfamiliar. I'd like to bring it in to the shop, clean it up and examine it more closely."

"I don't feel that would be my decision but I can ring up Stephen or Thomas from the library."

"Good, it's just that the desk has built up stains and could use a good cleaning.

"You're right of course and I'm sure they will be in favor, but I still have to ask."

In the library, I use the landline phone to call the mill office.

"This is Thomas." Rather abrupt for Thomas I think.

"Thom, Ted Peyton is here from Village Antiques and would like to take the desk into the shop to clean it and possibly date it, is that alright?"

"Hold on a second, Dad's here with our engineer." I hear him talking in the background.

"Ok with us both. Just warn Ted he'll need to bring a crew with him to get it down. Thanks Sarah." I hear the click at the other end signifying the abrupt end of our conversation.

"We're good." I assure Ted. "When do you want to do this?"

"How about next Tuesday, say around nine?" He asks.

"That would be fine. Thomas wanted me to remind you to bring a crew along to move it down to the truck since we have no one here to help."

"Don't worry, I'll have plenty of help, we move large pieces like this nearly every day," Ted assures me. "Sarah, lovely to meet you and don't forget to stop by the shop someday soon, okay?"

"I've actually been waiting for the rain to clear, but it doesn't look like that'll be soon." I tell him.

"That's right; if you're going to assimilate the U.K. life, you'll have to go it, rain or no." We laugh together as I acknowledge, "I'm beginning to realise that." We walk together to the door.

"Good bye Ted, see you Tuesday."

When I turn, Thomas is standing at the door of the library.

"You needn't have made the trip up here Thom; I know you are very busy."

"I came to give Ted my regards but see he's already left."

"He had some interesting things to say about the medals and the desk. Come into the library and sit for a minute and I'll tell you what we have so far."

"This is actually a nice break in a very long morning." Thom says as we sit in front of the fire. "Sorry if I cut you short earlier but our engineer for the Mill is in and we were in the middle of a design discussion."

"No problem, I sensed you were busy, but I didn't feel I had the right to decide if the desk was to leave the premises or not."

"I absolutely appreciate your caution, Sarah and you can always call me or my father whenever you have questions." He sits back to relax then asks, "What about the medals?"

"Ted believes the one is an India Service medal by the color of the ribbon. The other, the older of the two, is from New Zealand. Both are much worn and we were unable to read the engravings on their backs except for bits and pieces. Ted took pictures of both and will research them for us."

"I hope he has some luck." He stands up to leave. "I need to get back, but I'll see you later?"

"Yes, of course." I watch him walk down the hall.

« »

The library catalogue is finally finished and I turn from my desk. Berty left me a sandwich and glass of milk on a tray earlier which enabled me to continue working through the afternoon. It's taken a week to complete the library's inventory on the family and one thing is clear, the old tax records for the Estate show Stephen's name as owner in 1976 and Charles as early as 1940, but there are no records prior to that.

After dinner I resume my research, but yawn as I realise the time and put the computer to sleep. Another day gone, how quickly the past eighteen days have flown for me. Before leaving the library I make a note to ask Stephen about his father's letters tomorrow, any other files stored for taxes prior to 1940 and any existing house plan drawings.

A hot shower would be heavenly I think as I enter my room and walk directly to the bathroom. Then, showered and in pajamas, I towel-dry my hair and let Tom out before calling it a night. He leaves without hesitation, probably in search of Missy.

Monday evening everyone waits around the table in the kitchen for "American Fare" night as I enter.

"Sarah, we were beginning to wonder if you'd forgotten our food contest" Stephen says as I grab a chair at the table.

"I'm late, so sorry everyone; please, let's get started. Jamie, that pizza smells heavenly. And those burgers — let me at 'em!" It seems so long since I've bitten into one, I think.

An hour later all the pizza has been eaten and one burger remains. Stephen makes short work of his second piece of pizza then announces, "Jamie, that was wonderful and Sarah, thank you for your suggestion."

"Anyone interested in retiring to the great room?" Thomas asks.

"Please say no dancing tonight," I beg with a smile, "and I'm there."

"Very well, in lieu of dancing, Jamie please pull out the good brandy and bring it upstairs. We'll see just how good it really is."

Everyone cheers and we walk upstairs where Berty has already lit the fire and turned on some of the lamps in the room. We sink into the sofas and chairs to enjoy the evening.

I watch my 'family' get settled and reflect that soon I will be bound back home to the States; my preliminary work is almost complete and the remainder can continue via computer from home. I'm not sure how I feel about leaving Highbridge and the lovely people here.

"What's wrong Sarah?" Thomas asks softly so the rest won't hear.

"The inevitable trip back home is coming up. I'm just realising I'll miss all of you."

"And I...we will miss you as well." He replies.

"You know at some point you will need to begin working with a genealogist in Europe who knows the record resources of this country." I tell him.

"Will you at least stay until I've found that person?" he begs with a smile.

"Of course, I'll make sure you're set to continue before I go back."

"Ok you two, over here please and help us sample this fine brandy." Stephen calls and we join him in front of the fire with the others.

"Here's to family past and present." Everyone lifts their glasses.

The next morning I learn that a headache can result after one glass of brandy. I roll carefully out of bed, taking a moment to steady my throbbing head then walk slowly to the bathroom where I find aspirin and take two with tap water.

At the closet I throw on sweat pants, a warm sweater and sneakers. Giving my hair a couple of swipes, I glance into the mirror and realise it is totally out of control. I stuff some renegade tendrils behind my right ear. This is as good as it gets folks I say to myself and walk to the door.

Down in the kitchen three people look in much the same condition and sit with their heads hanging over their coffee cups.

"Ok, just to put it on record here, this is all Thomas' fault." I joke despite my head and walk to the counter for coffee.

"Oh no, no. Let it be recognized that it was Sarah who said 'no dancing' and therefore it rested upon me to choose alternative entertainment." He states quietly and conceals his smile.

Everyone replies "Here-Here." then regrets it as we hold our aching heads.

"Alright I see how it is, but could you-all keep it down low please." I implore them.

Jamie brings me a glass of something red with a lime section in it and says "drink this." I look at it then drink it. Tomato juice with a twist of lime—actually tastes good.

"Thanks Jamie for not adding what's usually in these."

"No problem, hair of the dog is an old wives' tale and not what you need; you're just dehydrated. Now, anyone want sausage and eggs?"

We answer with a resounding "No."

I bring my coffee along to the library and feel somewhat better as I wait for Ted's arrival. Punctual at nine am, he brings along a crew of five men. It takes them an hour to work the desk around the various stairwells from the attic, to the widest stairway to the entry door on a dolly. The desk, once outside is easy to load onto the truck's hydraulic tailgate.

Ted walks to me for a signature on the receipt.

"How's your father?" I ask him.

"He'll live I think," he jokes, "he's always had a talent for feeling worse than anyone else in the world when he's sick, even my mother agrees. I'll give him your regards."

"Please do." I wave goodbye and watch the truck proceed out the driveway. As I walk back to the house, I see Thomas upstairs and wave.

≪≫

From the upstairs window I watch as the desk is loaded safely into the truck then see Ted come back to Sarah for a signature. They laugh together and I wonder what it could be about. She waves at me and I smile, raising my hand to her greeting.

Is Ted interested in her I wonder...and if he is, what am I going to do about it?

I walk the back hallway and retreat out the back door for my day at the mill office without an answer.

≪≫

Chapter 6 Secrets

"The New Zealand Cross, Sarah," Ted reports to me over the phone this morning, "was first awarded in 1869 for service in the New Zealand land wars to both military and colonial volunteers." He sounds rather excited at the discovery and so am I.

"The date of service and the name of the person awarded were by design," he continues, "engraved on the back of each arm of the cross. I know the medal is badly worn and damaged on the reverse and neither of us noticed anything readable; but you should take another look to be sure we didn't miss anything at least partially visible."

"You're right Ted. Let me look at them again and I'll call you right back."

In the library, I pull out the medals and turn over the one from New Zealand. I can barely make out a date but if I had to guess, it would be "1869"; the name is almost totally obliterated. I try again using the library's lighted magnifying glass and think I can see a faint engraving of the name 'Smith'.

Trembling as I open and examine the India General Service medal, indeed it's badly worn but I can see a partial date of "19__" and a few letters; "R__ An__". The rest has been taken away by time and abuse.

I call Ted back and give him the information; he promises to keep working for further info on the award of both medals.

This is our first real "aha" moment and I can't wait to find Thomas to tell him in person. I'm down the staircase to the back door when I notice Jamie in the kitchen.

"Have you seen Thomas this morning?"

"He and Mr. Stephen are at the construction office." He replies.

"Thanks. I'm going out for a walk and chase off some of my cabin fever."

"The weather out there should do that," He calls as I grab a slicker from the hook. I sit under the entry overhang to pull on wellies and pick up an umbrella then step outside.

The rain continues to fall, though a little lighter and finer than in previous days, I hoist the umbrella and follow the wet walkway around the house. After weeks inside, the cool dampness is exhilarating.

John and his crew have been busy; the flower beds and roses around the house are trimmed back and neatly mulched in for the months of winter ahead. Two magpies sit on top of the garage and loudly voice their 'opinions' across the yard, their white 'vests' and wing feathers visibly bright in the day's general gray color. I look up to

146

the woodland trees shed of their colorful leaves and branches here and there populated by mistletoe; they otherwise stand stark against the sky. Bushy evergreens show their green as they thrive in the cool, rainy weather and stand strong in the leafless forest; though I am too far away, I know their fragrance is high. In front of the house several tiny chaffinches dart among the wet cedars overhanging the driveway, busily finding insects which have taken shelter in the branches.

Thomas and Stephen discussed over dinner last night how they were looking forward to the foundations being set in place this morning; I hope the weather hasn't made them postpone their plan. The gravel lane down to the site is a little trickier than 'bumping down' in the old Rover and I watch my step in the slick gravel on the hill. I'm a bit chilled by the time I reach the construction office and take down my "brolly" to shake and lean it against the building.

"Whew." I exhale as I step inside the door and quickly close it against the weather. I turn with a smile to see Thomas and Joe look up at me in surprise from the blueprints on their table.

« »

"Sarah; what in the world are you doing here?" I help her remove her waterproof and give her a towel from behind the door to dry her face.

"Why didn't you call, I would have come up to the house." I have to smile though at the enjoyable sight before me; auburn hair damp with the rain outside curling all over the place and her face flushed from the chilly air, quite a beautiful sight.

"Oh Thom, it wasn't necessary, I needed to get out for some exercise. Hello Joe." She calls to my partner at the draft table.

"Good morning Sarah," Joe answers, "looks like you're handling this weather just fine. Would you like some tea, we have a pot over here?"

"That's sounds lovely, yes I would. Sorry to interrupt you both, but Ted called this morning with some news. Where's Stephen?"

"He went into the Village to interview applicants for the farm manager position. We postponed further foundation work, so he thought he'd take advantage while he had the time. What's the news?" I ask.

"The medal Ted couldn't identify right away is called a New Zealand Cross and it dates back to 1869." I watch Thom's expression change as he processes my words.

"Wow...why would it be in that trunk, in our house?"

"Yes, well that's the question isn't it?" She replies. "Here's the kicker; the initials on its back are badly rubbed out but I think the name of Smith may be visible. And the rest of the puzzle, the other medal is also badly worn but I can see a partial date containing "19" and the letters "R" and "An". Obviously both medals are pertinent to your family history somehow, we just have to determine how and who."

"Can we do that?" I ask her.

"I think there are military records with lists showing the dates of award and Ted is on the trail for additional info. I'm going to query the internet when I return to the house, but I just wanted to give you this news myself." Sarah has taken the proffered cup of tea from Joe and has her hands wrapped around it as she sips.

"Thank you for braving the weather like this," I tell her. "Now that you're here, would you like to see the additions that Joe has proposed for the mill?"

"I would love that Thomas if we can make it brief, I'm anxious to get back to my computer."

"No problem, we'll be brief." I assure her with a smile and clear a stool at the table. "We're thinking of putting a small café in the plans including a terrace for dining during the warmer months. Patrons will be able to watch the wheel turn as they enjoy their food."

"Really," Sarah says in surprise, "I never thought of a mill with a café."

"Yes, we think it might be a place for visitors to sample and buy our products; give us some increased revenue, perhaps even pull some tourist trade in." I add.

"You know eventually, we could go to online product sales, too." Joe says.

"It sounds like a place that would be popular. Are you prepared to have your privacy disappear though?" Sarah asks. "Once people see how beautiful it is here, they may just want to take a walk around to see the house and grounds."

"I've thought of that and it's something Dad and I will need to discuss; I don't know where he'll stand on any of this yet. At any rate, we'll include the café and it could be repurposed later if need be." I tell her.

Stephen blusters through the door and greets us as his overcoat drips on the mat. "Good heavens, it's not fit for anyone with half a brain out there."

I smile at him, "Well, that would include Sarah I suppose."

"Yes, she walked down here from the house for the exercise." Joe relates.

"Well, well, you're turning into a true Brit. But let me drive you back up. I'm going there anyway." Stephen says.

"That's an offer I'll accept and on the way I can fill you in on this morning's news." Sarah tells him.

"News?" He questions as he helps her into her slicker. She turns from the door to look back at me and Joe, "See you boys later at dinner?"

"We'll be there, Joe's staying as well." I tell her.

"Wonderful, see you then."

« »

While Stephen drives, I tell him about the medals and what Ted found on them.

"How mysterious, Sarah; I've never heard anything like this before in our family. Hopefully you or Ted will be able to shed more light on their recipients," He says.

A wonderful smell welcomes Stephen and I at the kitchen door; Jamie has prepared lunch and his vegetable-beef soup simmers on a back burner. We can't resist and sit down to consume two helpings of the warming brew.

"Stephen, do you know of any drawings from the original construction of this house?" I ask.

"I remember some as a child. They were in my father's library and I believe they were in a large portfolio binder. I haven't seen them since and wouldn't know where to start looking, providing they are still even in existence."

"What do you mean? Would someone remove them from the library?" I ask.

"No, no, I don't think so, but paper doesn't last very well in this climate with the dampness and all." Stephen finishes his soup with a final slurp from the edge of the bowl.

"Well, it's worth a look-through and I guess, in addition to my computer search for the medal, I'll add a 'library search party' session as well." I'm very excited at the idea.

"Why not borrow Berty from his household duties for a few hours and have him search the higher shelves my dear," Stephen asks. "I don't want you falling off one of those high ladders."

Emily joins us at the table and Stephen takes advantage to suggest, "Emily, could you provide Berty some time in the library for Sarah? She's looking for some drawings of the house and will need help with the higher shelves."

"No problem sir," Emily says, "I have him in the attic with some cleaning but I'll send him round shortly; he'll probably be happy to leave it for a while." She turns to me next.

"I have you to thank for bringing me up there Miss Sarah, it was such a mess; I didn't realise how the dust had accumulated." Emily leaves the table, but pauses to remind us, "Don't forget we're having dinner in the dining room for a change. Mr. McHugh is coming and bringing his wife Dorothy," then she rushes away back to the attic.

"I'm sure Berty is glad you brought her up there with you, Sarah." Then he winks, "And he'll be grateful you've given him a little break from it, too."

I laugh, "Poor man, I'd forgotten about Em's cleaning skills. By the way, have you had a chance to read through those letters we found in the trunk?"

"I've glanced at several, but with the mill and farm plans taking so much of my day, I haven't given the letters the attention they deserve. I promise I'll finish them up this week and report back to you."

Berty checks in with me at one-thirty in the library and I describe to him what we are looking for.

"The house plans could be folded to a smaller size and placed in a regular bound file, or stored in their original size in a loose portfolio. If the latter, they might be on top of the cabinets since they wouldn't fit on a shelf, so please start up there and I'll go for the lower shelves."

"Yes Miss." Berty replies and climbs a ladder to search the shelves closest to the door while I start at the lower shelves on the other side of the room.

Two hours later, neither of us has found the drawings and I call a fifteen minute rest break. When I return, Berty has placed a tray on the table with tea and cakes on it from the kitchen.

"Oh Berty, how did you know? It's just what the doctor ordered. Please, join me." I invite him.

"Thank you Miss Sarah, climbing ladders does tend to burn off one's lunch." He reaches for a cake before returning to the ladder.

I work my way around the room to the last shelf unit on the west side of the library and shine my flashlight along the row of books on the third shelf. I stop as I notice something strange; the edge on the middle of the shelf is uneven and on closer exam it seems to be split through the shelf's surface. I rub my fingers along the wood and feel a definite divide, so I decide to remove the books from the shelf and examine it more closely.

When I pick up two books I hear a "click" followed by some sort of squeak from under the shelf itself. I immediately stand back and call "Berty!" as the shelf drops down and away, leaving a dark, musty-smelling space where it had been. He comes quickly and together we stare into the space, trying to adjust our eyes to its darkness and the smell of mold and age.

I pick up my flashlight and shine it into the void. The back wall of the compartment is several feet in, its sides at either end of the shelf. On its bottom is some sort of package and other objects which I start to reach for, but at the last minute decide not to.

"Berty, go and call Thomas and Stephen, they need to be here." and I step back. My heart is pounding; I've never experienced anything like this—ever. My hopes are high at this moment that all will be revealed for Stephen and Thomas' sakes. But as I gain control, I prepare myself for the worst as well; what if we find documents stored for security, which have nothing to do with family history?

I make myself sit down at the tea tray and pour a cup despite the fact that my hand rather shakes. I feel more in control of my emotions after a few sips and wait for Stephen and Thomas.

They practically run into the room as both were down in the kitchen when Berty found them and told them what had happened.

Stephen scans the room and sees the dark space in the shelves.

"Good heavens," he says excitedly and walks over to it with Thomas on his heels. "I've never seen this before."

Thomas brings the large floor lamp from across the library and places it close to the shelf so that the light can shine directly into the space. When he turns it on, all four of us crowd around to have a look.

There are four visible items inside and Stephen starts to remove them one by one and hand them to Thomas. Berty clears the tea table of its tray and brings it closer for Thomas to place each item on it. There are actually six packages in all with two smaller boxes found inside the dark corners of the space. Each is wrapped in oil cloth and tied.

"This is an old method used years ago as an attempt to prevent dampness from seeping inside," I say as I touch one of the packages to see what condition the wrapping is in, "it seems to be intact."

When Stephen is satisfied nothing remains, we turn our attention to the table's display. I bring out my camera and take pictures of the space as well as the items on the table.

"Who would like to unwrap these presents?" I glance around at them with a smile.

"You do it Sarah." Stephen directs, "my touch is pretty rough and I don't want to damage anything inside these." I turn to Thomas who nods.

"Very well," I agree and wait while Thomas cuts the knotted string that binds the first and largest package. I carefully pull back each corner of the oiled cloth wrapping and find a stack of parchment sheets, which appear to be the plans to Highbridge, all in very good shape.

"Wonderful; I would love to pour my attention into these, but let's move on. Berty, could you put these over on the library table so that we can examine them later."

I open the second bundle with Thomas' help and inside a paper wrapper is what appears to be a sort of agreement, signed and registered in Aberdeen Scotland from the looks of the seal on the bottom of the last page. The longhand script is unintelligible; we can't read the names or dates on the document which looks to be partially moisture damaged.

"Any ideas gentlemen," I ask. Stephen and Thomas both hold up their empty hands in astonishment.

I take pictures of the document and then hand the package to Berty. "Let's move on."

In one of the largest packages I find what might be a land agreement because there are coordinates written in the wording of the document. We all look at each other then I notice something.

"Look here; these coordinates were on the other document as well." Thomas checks and confirms it.

When the fourth package lays open, it again appears to be a legal agreement between four people in a language we don't recognize. There are signatures at the bottom, one last name appears to be a Smith, but the rest are unrecognizable due to moisture damage. The document stamp however, is very familiar.

"The shell," Thomas sees it first.

"I think we have plenty to research now, don't you?" I ask with a wide grin on my face. "Let's finish up and decide where we want to go next, shall we?" and I carefully take the last document over to the table.

The two smaller boxes remain; one gives up an item that explains a lot. It's a heavy brass stamp used to seal correspondence and documents; when I turn it over, I hold it up and ask, "Recognize this?"

Stephen exclaims, "It's the same design on my father's watch fob and on the trunk."

"And on the last documents," Thomas adds, "Have you considered it may not have been your father's watch fob, but his father's or his grandfather's?"

"Good point." I agree, "We need to get some experts involved in this and come up with some interpretation on these documents." I remember something I recently read and ask, "Anyone with ties to Aberdeen University? I've read they have an excellent antiquities department; maybe they'd like to do some pro bono work for us."

"Excellent idea, Sarah," Thomas says. "I have a friend there who attended university with me, Donald Ferguson. I'll give him a call when we finish here."

"We've forgotten the last box." Stephen holds up the small case and hands it to me. "Would you like to do the honors, Sarah?"

"I would love to," I unwrap the box, lift its lid and gasp in surprise. There nestled in blue velvet are the pearl earrings and brooch I'd seen in the dining room portrait; they belonged to Alicia, Stephen's mother. I look up at Stephen and hand them to him. He's speechless and takes the box to sit in one of the overstuffed chairs by the windows.

"Shall we cover all of this up for now?" I ask. "Berty, could you bring an old sheet or dustcover?" He leaves for the linen room to retrieve one.

Thomas turns and surprises me by saying "I think I need a hug." I consider it a second then step into his arms, wrapping mine around his neck.

He releases me after a few seconds and I look at him. "I needed that too," I say. "This is wonderful stuff we've discovered today and I'm quite shaken by it all. How does it feel to have your past opened up?"

"More important to me is how it feels to him." Thomas nods at Stephen who looks up from the box in his hands. "Well Dad?"

"It's like a door has opened that's been closed for a very long time. When I see these I remember my mother as she actually existed in my life and it's a very good feeling. Thank-you, Sarah."

"You are welcome Stephen."

"This calls for a celebration." He changes his mood to one of utter happiness.

"We're having a dining room dinner tonight and I think it should be something special in honor of my mother and father and whoever else is back there in time." He jumps up from the chair, "I'm going down to see Jamie." And with that, Stephen disappears around the side of the doorway into the hall.

« »

Sarah and I both burst into laughter at Dad's boisterous exit. "Now you see where I get my periodic fits of energy," I tell her.

Berty comes back with a dust cover and we place it over the table and its contents.

"I'm going upstairs to get cleaned up Thom," Sarah says, "see you at dinner."

"Yes, I look forward to it," I tell her and return to my room to do the same.

Shortly after doing so, I hear a knock at my door.

"Dad, anything wrong?" I ask then step aside as he enters.

"No actually, everything is perfect this evening son. I just want to talk to you about something I noticed today in the library.

"Ok, let's sit down." I pull out two chairs to the fireplace.

"I noticed you and Sarah in an embrace today after all our discoveries."

I feel a flush across my face. "That was just a thing, sort of a celebratory hug in honor of her discoveries in the library, that's all Dad."

"I noticed you two the other night having a small conference on the other side of the great room."

"Yes, we were talking about her eventual return to America after her project here is finished."

"I also saw you two waltzing in the great room with each other last week."

"Yes, well it is hard to waltz alone and not nearly as much fun. What's this all about Dad?"

"I just want to make sure where you're headed with these little nuances Thomas, that's all. Sarah is a wonderful woman; she's been through much sorrow early in life and she deserves no more during the rest of her life," Then turning back to the fire he asks, "Do you agree?"

"Look Dad," I rise from my chair in discomfort, "I'm not ready to admit this to anyone but you, understand? I have feelings for Sarah and have had since I met her at university when Brian introduced us. She truly loved Brian and didn't even remember me when I contacted her about our family's genealogy. Seeing her again has brought back those feelings I experienced when they were pointless. I have no illusion that she cares for me now and I don't want to complicate the situation by believing we have a chance. We live on different continents and I doubt either of us is ready to join the other in a change of life style."

"I respect that son, but listen to me on this one piece of advice, please. Don't make the mistake of keeping your feelings secret from her." I prepare to interrupt, but he continues.

"If you do, Thomas, you'll live with regret for the rest of your life that you didn't find out how it could have turned out, do you hear me?"

"Yes, I hear and I'll take your advice out of respect for you, Dad, but I can't promise it will change anything."

"Fair enough son, See you at dinner?"

"Yes, and Dad...thanks." He pats me on the back as he passes.

"Now I must call Joe and Dorothy about tonight's dinner plans and apologize for the short notice on dress. I want this to be a dinner in honor of family present and past and we're all dressing up. See you downstairs son."

I pull out my dinner jacket after Dad leaves, a little apprehensive since it hasn't been worn for several years. Emily has apparently had it cleaned since my arrival back home, thank goodness for her. Only Dad and Jamie could arrange an entire formal dinner for the same day, but it is wonderful to see Dad so enthusiastic.

« »

"Hello Dorothy, it's Stephen. How are you? Yes, quite fine thank you; looking forward to having dinner with you and Joe tonight. Good, good. One little detail which I hope won't ruin it for you, well, we had some surprising discoveries in the library today regarding the genealogy research Sarah's been doing and I've decided to make tonight's dinner a celebration in the old style and dress for dinner. What do you think? Really? Splendid; dressed to the nines you say? Thank you so much for being tolerant of an old man's short planning. Yes, yes, see you this evening. Goodbye."

I turn from the phone and retrieve my jacket from the wardrobe. Thank heaven it still fits, I might have put on a pound or two around the middle and I stand back to observe the full effect in the mirror. Satisfactory, I think to myself, after all, I am getting older.

I take a red rose from its vase Emily thoughtfully placed here earlier, snap the stem and put the bud in my lapel in memory of mother's love of roses. I realise my heart is fuller and more alive than I've felt in years and for the first time in a long while, I walk down to the great room with anticipation for the evening.

After pouring myself a small glass of wine I turn to see Meggs and think to myself she's looking lovely and it occurs to me, perhaps it's through new eyes I see her tonight.

"Good evening Stephen, don't you look distinguished in your formalwear."

"Thank you, I was just thinking the same of you. Won't you join me in a glass of wine?"

"I would love to." We turn as Thomas joins us.

"Look at you two, didn't know there would be royalty here tonight," my son quips.

Before we can rally with a reply, Berty brings in Joe and Dorothy and we make them welcome. I happen to look at Thomas but he seems mesmerised by something behind us. I follow his gaze to the top of the stairs where Sarah pauses to look down at our guests.

« »

I see her above the room as she hesitates before coming down the staircase. Sarah wears a long, soft gray dress with fine silver chains at her neck. Her auburn hair in ringlets around her face touches her shoulders and I think I've never seen a woman more beautiful. I seem to be glued to this spot, unable to move and glance over at Stephen who winks at me.

« »

"Good evening Sarah." Stephen comes to greet me and leads me by the hand to Joe and his wife.

"Dorothy, may I introduce Sarah Sandlin; Sarah, this is Dorothy McHugh, Joseph's wife."

"Hello, so nice to meet you. Stephen tells me you both live nearby," I remark.

And so the conversations begin, with Dorothy and I getting acquainted and sharing a little wine before Berty calls us in to dinner.

I catch my breath at how lovely the dining room looks. All the chandeliers are lit, the china and glassware sparkle and Stephen has had several vases of fresh red roses placed down the table in honor of his mother.

"How beautiful," I remark to him, "I'll bet Emily had something to do with this."

"Yes Sarah, she helped get it all together in a short amount of time, especially the red roses. She earned a raise today for sure." He laughs and turns to his guests.

"Please be seated everyone." Stephen says and pulls out a chair for Megg on his right.

Thomas seats me at the opposite side of the table from him, after whispering that he wants to see me the entire evening with no problem. I feel myself blushing as he moves one of the flower vases lining the table's center a

164

little to the left just to ensure a clear view. I try to be nonchalant about it but am flattered by his attention.

When wine is poured, Stephen stands and taps his glass to get everyone's attention. He briefs us on the discoveries made earlier in the library for Joe and Dorothy's benefit then proposes a toast as he turns to face the two portraits on the wall behind him.

"To my dear mother and father who raised me with love and endowed me with this home; and to my dear wife Alicia" he pauses, "who married me and gave me my son Thomas. May all be remembered well in this house and may their memory be joined shortly by that of others before them." Everybody responds with a "Here - Here" and we sip from our glasses.

Berty and Jamie serve a sumptuous feast; to everyone's astonishment, there are lobsters from the North Sea, thick steaks from the local butcher shop, fresh vegetables in a lemon sauce and creamy potatoes on the side with fresh-baked bread in small loaves for each guest.

Time and conversation flow easily and wine glasses are refilled as the evening's repast is enjoyed and consumed.

Stephen invites, "Come, my friends to the great room for brandy (I groan) and he adds, "and some of Jamie's excellent coffee" then escorts Meggs away from the table. The great room is ablaze with light and both fireplaces are lit to keep off the chill of the rain outside. Berty brings the brandy for the men and coffee for the ladies at our request.

"When do you expect to return to America?" Dorothy asks me.

"I think in about two weeks. We do have a little more to complete on this project now, in view of today's find. Dorothy, were you born and raised here?" I ask her.

"Oh goodness no, I'm from Massachusetts." She laughs.

"Massachusetts—I thought there was something different about your accent."

"Yes, Joe and I met at MIT. He graduated and went back to London. In six months he came to my doorstep on one knee with an engagement ring." She smiles wistfully.

"It must have been quite a decision to leave all you knew for a foreign country." I remark.

"I don't know that I could have done that, my dear." Megg tells Dorothy.

"Well, truthfully I loved him so, I would have gone anywhere he wanted me to," Dorothy glances over at Joe, "and still would," She adds. "When I first came to Britain, we lived with his parents at their place until Joe landed his mill job in Edinburgh."

"How long were you there?" I ask.

"We stayed until we saved enough for a farm, about ten years then moved back here to be near Joe's parents. They were getting on and we knew his Dad would need someone to farm his land for him pretty soon. We've been here since 1950 and never regretted it."

"So you never used your degree?" I remark.

"I've written several books on farm engineering, time studies, use of best equipment, etc.; they're mostly used at schools and universities. It's something I can do from home and I've been happy at it."

"And you Megg, where did you meet your husband?"

"We met in Kent, Sarah. He was a fine, handsome man and had a little tailor shop that catered to the upper classes. He learned to sew while in the military and provided a good living for us."

"Do you have any children?" Dorothy asks Megg.

"Yes, I have a daughter and grandchildren down in York. My husband died in 1990 of heart trouble. It took many years before I learned to live again, but I did. One day I realised that Douglas would not want me to live apart from this wonderful world and all that it offers. So I looked for a job and Smith Imports hired me as a secretary. That's where I've spent the years and they've gone by quickly. But they were good years and now look at me. I feel like I'm retired and living the life. Stephen is a wonderful man to work for and his wife, bless her, was such a support to him. After she passed, he completely lost himself in his work."

Meg turns to look across the room at Stephen who's laughing at some joke with the men. "He's happier than

I've seen him in many a year. I think he has both you and Thomas to thank, Sarah." She places her hand on mine. "I add my thanks for that as well."

The evening draws to a close as Joe and Dorothy make their way to the door and wish all a good evening.

"Sarah, let's get together soon for a lunch, shall we?" Dorothy invites me before following Joe out the door.

"Yes, I'd love that."

"Good, I'll call you next week." She says.

Stephen and Thomas wave them off and both head upstairs for some much-needed rest. Megg also takes her leave saying her goodnights and I am left to walk back into the great room where I decide to enjoy the quiet and watch the flames in the fire a little longer before turning in.

« »

From the second floor rail I see Sarah sitting by the fire and decide to return downstairs.

"May I join you?" I ask her.

"Of course Thomas, but I'm only here for a little while; I'm afraid wine makes me sleepy."

I sit down beside her then bend to take off her shoes, and set them aside.

"And why did you do that?" She asks.

"That's what most women would like to do at the end of the evening but don't want to seem improper." I tell her.

"You know you're right, thank you Mr. Smith. And what do most men want to do, but don't want to seem improper?"

"Sarah...this man wants to kiss you." I say softly.

She stops smiling and looks at me.

"Then, you'd best do it while you have the chance Mr. Smith," she says and waits for me.

I lean to her and touch her face for the first time. I kiss one cheek lightly then playfully kiss her nose before going on to slowly capture her warm lips with mine. She responds and I feel her kiss deepen, its warmth filling the emptiness inside me.

After several seconds I stop to look at her and see that her eyes are closed. I know I could do much more, but I stop because there are questions that can't be answered tonight; but perhaps tomorrow.

《 》

I open my eyes and see Thomas has left me and stands with one hand extended in invitation, my shoes in his other.

"Come on, I'll walk you home," He says and together we walk up the stairs and he leads me to my door.

"Good night Miss Sarah." He says, but I turn to him. He doesn't seem to think about it twice and kisses me again. This time all playfulness is gone and it's the most natural thing in the world to receive his kiss.

He pauses, and I tell him, "You're pressing your luck Mr. Smith."

"See you in the morning." He says and strokes my cheek with the back of his hand then walks away.

I open the door and close it behind me with a deep sigh. Of course Tom just makes it inside and jumps to the bed.

"Well mister, looks like it's just you and me; story of my life." I lay down just for a minute to pet him. When I open my eyes again, it's nine am. Breakfast is history and I realise I'm still in my clothes from the night before—again.

After a hot shower I dress and take a walk down the front stairs to escape for a while outside. Gathering my coat close in the early chill I take time to think about yesterday and to avoid thoughts on how it ended in the great room and at my door. I've always been good at avoiding subjects that make me nervous... especially Thomas. I walk via the side gardens around the end of the house in the general direction of the kitchen door.

The sun is actually shining this morning; the news did say the rain was expected to move off to France—Hallelujah. I look briefly down at the mill but there are no trucks or workers about, maybe they've taken a day to let everything dry off.

Tom and Missy are on their morning rounds together at the old horse barns and I laugh when they both crouch low to leap into action as one of the farm ducks approaches. But when the bird walks by as if they aren't there, they relax and pause to nonchalantly lick their paws before they continue their prowl.

I resolve to collect myself today and make a list of items to take care of before leaving for home. A reminder for Thomas to call his friend in Aberdeen to see about an assessment of the documents is first on the list and I wish to go along to Aberdeen and hear firsthand what the documents can tell us.

Secondly, I'll visit Ted in his shop and hear his thoughts on the desk. I can't help but think it's linked to Stephen's grandfather or even his great grandfather.

And thirdly, the New Zealand Cross and the India medal are both puzzles I need to solve, including who the medals were presented to and why they were stored here.

Those items considered, I come round to the subject of Thomas. He was so sweet to me last night, but I'm not blind enough to think that it was anything but the wine we both consumed at dinner and the brandy the men finished the evening with. No, don't let yourself make something out of this that it's not, I tell myself. And for heaven's sake, don't make it awkward for him in the days that remain of this visit. Just act normally and all will be well. With that little self-administered advice complete, I find myself at the kitchen door. Breakfast is long over and the kitchen vacant except for Jamie who sits reading the papers.

"Good morning, out for a bit of a stroll I see," He remarks.

"Yes, I needed to clear my head after last night's party which, by the way, featured some fantastic food thanks to you, sir."

"Thank you very much, Sarah. It did seem to please everyone and that's hard to do sometimes. Can I get you anything?"

"No thank you, I overslept so I'll just help myself to cereal and coffee until lunch, but thanks Jamie." I go to the pantry to retrieve the granola and pour myself a cup of coffee. "See, you've trained me well."

He smiles back then resumes reading the paper. "Oh I'm sorry, would you like part of this?"

"Just the funnies if you don't mind. I've missed them since I've been here."

"Here you go," he slides the newspaper section down the table.

I finish up both the funnies and my breakfast then push away from the table.

"Have you seen Thomas this morning?" I ask.

"I have; he came down around seven, had a couple of eggs said he had an early appointment and went to the garage. I don't know when he's expected back, but ask Miss Margaret, she may know more."

"Thanks Jamie, I will." I leave for the library and on my way, Berty approaches in the hallway.

"Hello Berty, have you seen Margaret?"

"Yes Miss Sarah, she's in the great room at her desk."

Megg looks up as I walk in. "Hello, how are you? We missed you at breakfast."

"Yes, quite a party and I was out like a light until nine am, but I feel fine now."

"Well, I slept late myself. I'm not used to late evenings, more of a morning person really."

"Megg, did Thomas say when he'd be back from his appointment?"

"Why no, but he went down to York, something about the mill, so he should be back this afternoon."

"What are you doing today Megg?"

"I have some work to do for Stephen but nothing that couldn't be done later, why do you ask?"

"I want to go to the Village today and see Ted at the antiques store regarding Stephen's desk. My curiosity is killing me."

"That sounds like a fun little trip to me, let's do it," Megg declares. "I have my car and we can stop at the bakery for tea if you like."

"Wonderful, thank-you Meggs, I'll just run upstairs for my purse and meet you in front."

When I come out of the house, Megg is already in the drive and we're off.

"I imagine you're glad to see the sun, being from Florida." She laughs.

"Actually we have a rainy season and of course there's hurricane season. What I miss most is my little yard with all its beautiful trees and flowers. I can't grow as many tropical plants as south Florida, but I still have my share of gardenias, lilies, orchids and such."

"Oh it sounds lovely. I've never been out of the U.K."

"Well, you'll have to come and visit me someday Megg, in fact, if you get vacation in the spring it's the prettiest time of year. We could go to the beach."

Megg laughs, "You may find me on your doorstep."

We arrive on the main thoroughfare of the Village and I look around with surprise at how many businesses there are in such a small place; a tailor, restaurant, bank, chemist shop and even an ice cream parlor.

Megg pulls up in front of the antiques shop and announces "Here we are."

We walk in and find Ted's father across the room, dusting some furniture.

"Hello Margaret, how are you, I haven't seen you here for some time," He greets her.

"Yes, I'm no longer collecting. You might say I've simplified my life now that I'm working with Mr. Smith at the Estate."

"That's wonderful Margaret, I'm so happy for you. And who's this lovely lady?"

"This is Sarah Sandlin from Florida. She's been at Highbridge helping with the family's genealogy research."

"Ah yes, Teddy brought Mr. Smith's desk back to the shop after you and I spoke over the phone; very nice to meet you Sarah." Mr. Peyton said and shook my hand warmly.

"Thank you. In fact, that's why we're here, I'm curious to see if he's uncovered any information yet?"

"Just a moment, I think he's in the back, I'll let him know you're here."

"Sarah, so good to see you;" Ted comes to greet us, "curiosity bring you by?"

"Yes, I'm afraid it did, I've never been good at waiting."

"Well, I do have news, as of yesterday. Please sit down, you too Miss Margaret" and he makes room at a large oak table, pulling out chairs for both of us.

"That desk hasn't been easy. You see the wood is strange to me, not from this area and not what I'm used to seeing. I have a friend who does carving and he uses a lot of exotic woods to do his craft, so when he stopped by the shop yesterday, I had him take a look."

"Did he recognize the wood then?" Meggs asks.

"Yes, it's Kauri wood. It may be from New Zealand, that's one of a few places in the south sea nations that it comes from... in the world."

"Then someone in the family lived for a time in the South Pacific; the evidence all points to it." I say with excitement.

"Certainly looks like it." He answers.

"Is there any sort of mark to tell us when or who made the desk?" I ask.

"There is not. And something else about Kauri wood; there's a unique chance this is ancient Kauri wood, that is, it may have been dug up from the northern New Zealand swamps. If it is, it can be over 45,000 years old and you can forget the age of the wood as a tool in your genealogy." Ted says.

"How is that possible?" Megg asks.

"There are Kauri farms producing new wood, but this desk may be from ancient wood, since it seems to have been in the Smith family for several generations. Kauri trees were major building material for ships and homes when settlers first came to the islands, so much so that they almost went extinct from overharvesting. Later, natives were known to dig up the old wood from the bogs for furniture makers. The mud in the bog preserved the wood for thousands of years after it sank into them. This desk may have been made for an English settler or more affluent customers such as the various governors, who rotated through the colonies, perhaps even shipped back here for Royalty.

"What an amazing story, I'm thrilled to hear this. You've been a great help, Ted, I can't thank you enough. You're going ahead with cleaning the desk, correct?" I ask him.

"Yes, Sarah, we'll take good care of the old girl and make sure she lives another forty-five thousand years."

"Thanks again. Just call us when 'she's' ready and we'll prepare a place of honor befitting her advanced age." I tell him.

"You are most certainly welcome...goodbye now."

Megg is as excited as I when we leave. "I can't believe this and to think Stephen had that wonderful desk up in the attic."

"I know Megg, wait until he hears this, he'll throw another party."

Meg turns to me outside the shop, "Shall we do a little shopping while we're here? There's a dress shop I've been dying to visit and haven't had anyone to do it with." She looks hopefully at me.

"I'd love it, let's go," I tell her and we walk arm in arm down the pavement.

We've arrived back at Highbridge just after four pm and Jamie already has tea set up in the kitchen. We just get settled for some cakes and tea when Stephen arrives.

"Well, the prodigals return. Where on earth have you two been?" He asks.

"Not that it's any of your business, but we've been shopping," I tell him with a smile.

"Yes and we spent money, if you must know." Megg follows my lead with a laugh.

Stephen pretends to be indignant. "Well I suppose you didn't think to buy me anything."

I put down my cup. "Well no, but we have some great information on your father's desk." I dangle the info in front of him and don't say more.

"Well, go ahead, tell me something; don't just stop." he sputters.

"The desk is made of Kauri wood from New Zealand and the wood may be over forty-five thousand years old." I look at Megg and then we both look at Stephen waiting for his reaction.

"Are you quite serious?" It takes some time to explain the day's events to him. Thomas comes in at the end of our story and wants to hear it all over again. Poor Megg excuses herself to get ready for dinner and Stephen leaves as well. I go over everything a second time for Thomas, who seems genuinely appreciative of Ted's help and we linger over a second cup of tea.

"I want to talk with you today about some things I'd like to do before my trip back home. Have you been able to contact your friend at Aberdeen?"

"No, I haven't. This meeting today took up all my time, but I'll give him a call tonight at his home."

"Good; Thom, would it be too much if I asked to make the trip there with you? I would really love to see Aberdeen while I have the chance and to hear what your friend has to say about the documents."

"I think it's an excellent idea, Sarah. I love road trips and they're entirely better with someone along who does, too." Then I notice his face turn serious.

"Sarah, I want to talk with you about last night," he says.

Well, there it is, I think; the one thing I didn't want to talk about.

"Last night? What about it?" I ask innocently.

"If my behavior was out of line, I'd like to apologize to you." Thomas says.

"Out of line? Surprising maybe, but not out of line. We both drank the wine at dinner and you and the boys had the brandy and we all know what that leads to." I finish lamely.

"What does it lead to?" He teases me.

"Why dancing of course. And taking off women's shoes without being asked and...other things."

"What other things?" He continues to tease me.

"Well for instance, kissing." I say and instantly feel like I'm sixteen years old again explaining my date at the prom to my father. It's too much and I scoot my chair out from the table.

"Ok, I'm going to the library to look at the documents again and prepare them to take to Aberdeen." I'm ready to dash from the room, but by the time I end my sentence, he is around the table and standing between me and the door.

"Sarah, please don't run away, I need to say something here and now. What happened last night was not planned, it was spontaneous and warm and honest and I would not take it back, even if you were angry." He stands firmly in front of me as he finishes his entreaty.

"Angry. Who said I was angry? I just don't want to talk about it and would like to go do the work that I was hired to do." I can feel my face blushing and hate that I sound so prissy.

"Then we're ok?" He asks.

"Yes, we're fine Thomas, now can I leave?"

"Yes, of course" and he steps aside. "I'll let you know as soon as possible about Aberdeen."

"Thank-you." I call from somewhere up the staircase.

《》

I wait a few minutes after Sarah leaves and try to make sense out of what just happened here, but can't. She sounded upset but said everything was fine.

I take my jacket and withdraw to the construction office. Thank heaven for daily work; a man could go crazy without it.

I finish up some entries to the books by 6 pm, close the computer then decide to call Don in Aberdeen before going up to the house for dinner.

The phone is picked up on the third ring and I hear a hearty "Hey there Thom." burst through on the other end.

"Don, how are you? Hope I didn't interrupt your dinner?" I say.

"No, not at all Thom, I just came in from the campus. How the heck are you and why don't you call more often man?"

"Right back at you." I say.

"Your Dad okay? Don asks. "I see both you and he have done some work moves over the last six months; tired of the same old same old?"

"That's pretty much what it was all about. You know, 'do it now or forever regret it', I admit.

"I hear you and don't think I haven't gone through the same. I'm still at the University but moved into research and history of this area about a year ago."

"Great, because I have a question for you," I tell him. "I brought over an American genealogist to help me find out more about my father's family."

"O yeah? Is she pretty?" Same old Don I think.

"Who says it's a 'she' first of all and secondly... yes, she is." I hear Donald burst into laughter.

"She's actually Brian Smith's wife." I add and hear the line grow quiet.

"Sarah? My gosh, how is she, I mean it's been how many years since..."

"Sarah is okay and it's been nine years. She lives in northern Florida and has a cat named Tom, which by the way came with."

"And...?" Don baits me.

"And I sort of like her."

"How old are you Thom, thirteen or thereabouts?"

"Alright, alright, I really like her. This is not why I called."

"Well ok, what can I do for you?"

"Sarah found some old documents inside a secret shelf in our library yesterday. Among them is something we think may be an agreement and it has an Aberdeen seal on the last page. But it's in some sort of dialect none of us is familiar with. It includes coordinates which are repeated on a second document. There are three documents altogether, but the third appears much older. All were wrapped in oil cloth and fairly well preserved but some of the text is moisture-damaged and blurred. We need someone who knows what they're doing and I thought of you."

"Sure, I'd be honored to take a look, how would you like to do this? I don't think I can get away very soon. Why don't you drive up with the documents, maybe we can have dinner after and talk over old times. What do you say?"

"Sarah will be coming along; I hope that isn't a problem?"

"No problem at all, I'd love to see her, do you think she'll remember me?"

"Probably not, she didn't remember me at first, so don't get your hopes up. How about Friday, day after tomorrow?"

"Actually, that would be perfect. I'm between terms and quite at my leisure," He says.

"Then we'll be there, probably get in around noon and I'll call you for your location."

"Great, see you then Thom."

I turn out the lights in the mill office and walk to the Rover. When I look up, the stars are bright and clear in the sky. A rare night with neither rain nor fog and I stop to breath in its crispness then think briefly about the past week's events and Sarah. I don't know exactly where this is going, but I hope the road trip will help us be more open with each other. If I find that she cares for me I will do whatever I can to meet her halfway in all things, except one; I can't possibly leave the U.K. or live anywhere else. My responsibility is to Dad and the Estate with its heritage so ingrained in me.

I enter the Land Rover and turn the key. Stupid to think Sarah would want to leave all that means anything to her in America and live in this damp, cold climate, rattling around in a house three times the size that any of us actually needs.

Later at dinner, I announce that Don Ferguson has agreed to take a look at our documents and that Sarah and I will be leave tomorrow morning on a road trip to Aberdeen.

"That's excellent news." Dad responds.

"We'll be gone overnight," I warn, "but we should return Saturday, late afternoon. No use trying to drive all the way up and back in 24 hours, especially if we take more time than expected at the University."

Dad agrees and Sarah echoes the same, adding "Oh my, I need to do some washing and decide what I'm going to wear. Please excuse me everyone."

She turns back at the stairwell to ask me "Thomas, is that Donnie Ferguson who went to school with you and Brian?"

Chapter 7 Road trip

The alarm clock goes off at six a.m. and I roll over quickly to shut it off. After a yawn and stretch, I struggle over the edge of the bed to grab my robe and walk to the bathroom.

The warm dress trousers and black sweater I laid out last night go on quickly and I pull out a warm black jacket and soft blue wool scarf picked up in the Village with Megg earlier this week. It was happenstance, I think, to find them before a road trip north to Scotland and it's bound to be a little chillier than here at the Estate. I pull on dress boots, grab my bag and walk down to get some breakfast.

Thomas is already eating oatmeal with some cinnamon toast that Jamie's placed for grabs from a hot plate. The smells in this kitchen are always wonderful, but at this hour, they're the best.

"Good morning." I say in general and help myself to oatmeal and coffee. "How are you Thom?"

"I'm fine and ready to get on the road. If we time it right, we'll miss the morning rush," He answers.

"Good plan, I look forward to seeing some scenery on the way," "I remark, "and Aberdeen looks amazing online, I can't wait to see it firsthand."

"I haven't been up for years," Thomas answers, "but it's about a six hour drive. I told Don I'll call him when we get to the city so he can give us directions to his location on campus."

We put on our jackets and Jamie hands Thomas a basket with a thermos of coffee, water, snacks and two sandwiches in case we miss lunch. "You can't go on a road trip without food," He insists and quickly throws in napkins and some handwipes.

"Jamie, you're the best," I tell him and give him a hug which makes him blush. "Go on you two, you'll be late," He says and walks back to the Aga range.

The car was warming up while we ate, so I remove my coat for the trip and put it on the back seat.

"I wouldn't mind taking turns driving, if you think you can trust me on the left side of the road," I suggest with bravado.

"Well, I can let you drive now while we're local if you'd like to get broken in," Thomas volunteers.

I hesitate then decide to try. We change places and I settle into the driver's side. Oh boy, this is definitely different. *Where's the headlight lever and the windshield wiper control?* I ask myself, but find them on opposite sides of the wheel to what I'm used to. This will take some getting used to. Thomas takes the time to walk me through all the particulars and adjusts the mirrors to fit my line of sight before I put the car in motion. I feel confident enough to at least drive to the end of the driveway.

Thomas is navigator so I don't have to worry about what direction to take and can concentrate on just driving.

"Go ahead and turn toward the village, I'll tell you ahead of time when to turn again," he says quietly.

All goes well on the highway until I see headlights coming our way in the right lane and I unconsciously slow. Thomas reminds me to stay in the left lane and the oncoming car will pass me on the right; indeed it does, much to my relief.

The next challenge comes at a stop sign just outside the village. When I turn left, I go into the right lane of the road instead of to the left lane. He reminds me to get to the left side of the road; luckily the road at this hour of the morning isn't busy.

"Oh Thom, do you want to take over, I'm not very good at this." I declare.

"No, I think this is good for you and you'll soon develop your Brit mentality when it comes to left and right."

So I practice my 'Brit mentality' for several miles before he decides we should trade driving duties again.

"We're nearly to the M6 highway and there'll be more traffic than you'll like." He says.

I smile at the terminology used to describe roads. M6 sounds like a type of gun to my tourist ears, but it is a clear description of one's location. With the merge onto A19 I feel happy I've given up the wheel and sit back to enjoy the trip.

"We'll take this to Newcastle then on to Edinburgh and across the River Forth Bridge. We have about an hour to Newcastle, so let me know if you need anything in the meantime, okay?"

"Thanks, I'm fine so far." My tablet is powered up to track our route as we progress and I like to look up area attractions as we pass by towns, even saving a couple for future reference.

"I love the round-abouts; we have very few in the U.S. and when one is built, it seems to take forever for people to use them properly. Do you know that in Clearwater, they actually had to tear one down because people were causing so many wrecks?"

"Yes, I imagine they do take some getting used to if you've never had them. It sounds comparable to my driving in New York with all the traffic lights and one way streets."

"Oh, you've been?"

"Once—I rented a car. Never again; Taxis ever after."

"Have you ever been around the U.K. and played the tourist?" I ask.

"I did take time in the summer between school and university," he tells me, "went by car from the east coast all the way around; I'd never had that kind of freedom before. Dad was pretty tough while I grew up and kept me on a short leash."

"He didn't trust you?"

"Yes, he trusted me, it was more a case of not trusting my friends," he laughs, "he took some of the choices away from me and became the "bad guy" so I could blame it on him."

"Quite a Dad isn't he." I say.

"He always knew what to do and the right way to do it without jeopardizing our relationship. I hope someday I'll be half the Dad he's been." Thomas admits.

"And you were an only child?"

"Yes, but not by choice; my mother had so much trouble during birth, the doctor said no more children. Dad told me they'd planned to fill up the house with kids, but it just wasn't to be. So they did the next best thing and welcomed children as often as they could to the Estate. When they hosted parties, parents were encouraged to bring their kids along instead of leaving them home with sitters. There would be these fantastic setups for them; ponies to ride, games on the lawn, everything they would've done for their own." Thom's eyes sparkle as he glances over to me.

"So is that why your Dad does the "scholarship" thing with the local youth?" I ask him.

"It is and he's been doing it since I completed university, look - we're almost to Newcastle." He adds. I look up everything I can find on the city.

"It says here that Newcastle is over 2000 years old," I tell him in amazement. "We have nothing but burial mounds to match that in the U.S.; a great number of historical buildings have been lost to disrepair or in the name of progress."

"Here now," Thomas responds, "there are some very lovely preserved historical sites in the U.S., you just don't have the longevity that we have here. Nor the number of takeovers this country has been through; Normans, Saxons, Romans, they've all been here."

"True," I admit, "and I do love my country; I just lose patience sometimes with the way we do things when it comes to preserving our history. If the money isn't there locally, it's sometimes very hard to get national funding."

Thomas agrees then adds, "You know, there's discussion right now in the U.K. on the practicality of constantly refurbishing our old buildings versus tearing them down and rebuilding with newer, better technology and materials. The cost is astronomical just to maintain them and we have so many."

"I can only imagine, but where will we Americans come to remember our roots? It just wouldn't be the same without the period architecture."

We stop at a petrol station in Newcastle on Tyne and take ten minutes to stretch and use the public toilet. There are so many wonderful buildings and the beautiful ultramodern bridge over the river Tyne. Had we time to spare, I would explore for hours, but we need to get back on the road and continue north.

"Next up is Northumberland National Park for about 30 kilometers on to Edinburgh," Thomas says. "By the way, keep an eye out for Hadrian's Wall before we enter the park. The Romans began building it about 122 AD and I think we'll pass by a portion of it."

"Got it." I continue to split my time between my tablet and the wonderful views all around. The day looks very promising and clear, a gift for our trip.

«»

I pull off at a small bistro before Edinburgh to stretch our legs and we order up a roast beef sandwich with hot mustard on whole wheat—to go, forsaking Jamie's sandwiches for something hot. Soon we are on our way again and as we merge onto the bypass around Edinburgh, I become aware that Sarah is extremely excited about being in the capital city.

"Do you see that oddly shaped mountain in the distance?" I ask her.

"Yes, what is that?" She asks.

"It's called Arthur's Seat and it's thought by some to refer to the real site of King Arthur's castle."

"But it's just a legend, isn't it?" She looks at me with some disbelief. "You are referring to the sword in the stone, Knights of the Round Table, etc. right?"

"Yes, I am and it's been very real to generations of believers and never been disproven," I say in defense. "They just haven't found the hard and fast evidence yet, but I secretly hope they do." I shoot her a smile.

"So you are a dreamer down there in that solid Brit soul." She smiles back and looks like the cat who swallowed a mouse.

"If that's what you want to call it then yes, I'm a dreamer," I admit, but she's still smiling at me.

"What?" I say sternly for effect then turn back to concentrate on the road ahead.

« »

Thomas continues to drive as we clear the beltway around Edinburgh and cross the bridge over the River Forth. We share the last of the roast beef sandwich and a bottle of water. I pick at one of Jamie's blueberry muffins and study the map on my tablet.

"We're making good time and we may be early," I say hopefully.

"We still have about three hours left and that's not including rest stops, so don't get overly confident Sarah-girl."

"Ok, I'll hold on to my optimism until we're closer. I'm surprised at the temperature though; I expected it to be chillier up here, but so far it's been maybe what, around fifty degrees?" I ask.

"You'll find that's normal for this time of year, as long as the wind doesn't bring in a storm off the North Sea, the climate stays pretty temperate. But you may need that coat and scarf for evening and early morning." He advises.

We're headed for Perth, where we'll turn briefly east to Dundee and drive the last hour or so north to Aberdeen. I notice several smaller towns between Dundee and Aberdeen, like Forfar and Brechin but the one I want to see on the coast is called Stonehaven. Its name evokes images of craggy bluffs with an old estate house clinging to its cliffs, like a scene from a Bronte novel, I think. I realise suddenly that Thomas is saying something to me and come back to reality.

"Sarah, are you alright? I've asked you something but you seem to be elsewhere."

"Oh I'm fine, just thinking about Stonehaven and what it must look like."

"And you think I'm a dreamer?" He teases.

We stop off in Perth for petrol and a rest stop and then wind around and back out on the other side of the

River Tay to catch the M90 again. In another fifteen minutes we've passed Dundee and are a little over an hour away from our final destination. *It will be good to stop moving,* I think as I shift in my seat.

"Getting to you?" Thomas asks, "I'm a little stiff myself and road-weary."

"Oh Thom, I know you must be, I wish I were a better driver."

"No worries, you will be, that is if you decide to come back for a visit someday." He quickly tries to cover his mistake, but too late, I've had a brief, but clear look at what Thomas is thinking. It really is too early to be thinking of 'us' and I gaze absently out the window.

« »

I notice she's left her tablet untouched during the last few miles and realise there is now indeed is a full-sized elephant in the car since I let slip my hope she will stay longer.

"Oh look, there's Stonehaven but we're too far out to see the town," she says, looking more than a little disappointed.

"Tell you what, if we leave a little earlier than planned tomorrow morning, we'll go into Stonehaven and explore; How about it?" I suggest to her.

"Oh, I'd love that." Sarah replies, "I could even take pictures like the full-fledged tourist that I am."

We drive into Aberdeen just before 1:30 and park at the University visitor's lot; both of us pull ourselves out of the car to stretch and walk a little.

« »

Some of the Kings College is visible and I study the sharp contrast of its older granite buildings to that of newer structures on the campus. Some, including a library building soon to be completed, are minimalist designs, popular in the 1950's.

Thomas puts in a call to Donald who assures us he'll come to retrieve us shortly and true to his word he arrives ten minutes after our call.

"Thom, you son of a gun, how are you?" he asks loudly as he grips him in a bear hug. "You look great, hanging around doing nothing all day must agree with you." He laughs and turns him loose.

"And Miss Sarah," he turns to me, "do you remember me?"

"Of course Donnie, how are you?" I extend my hand to him, which he immediately uses to pull me into the same hug Thomas has just escaped.

"You are beautiful as ever girl," He lets me go, but looks me over, "You haven't changed a bit; well, maybe better."

I can feel my face change to a rosy glow.

"So you do remember me?" Don says loudly, glancing sideways at Thomas.

"Why yes, why?" I answer.

"Well, it's just that Thomas warned me you might not since you'd already forgotten him when he first contacted you." Don has a devilish look in his eye.

I shoot a look at Thomas, "Oh did he?" I ask with promise of reprisal later.

"Okay, I see I'm outnumbered here and am changing the subject," Thomas says quickly. "How are Delores and the kids, Don?"

"They're wonderful, the kids are teenagers; Bri is sixteen and Duncan is seventeen. Delores has started her own business, she's a baker with a shop of her own, can you believe it?" Don says proudly.

He signs us both in and helps us obtain visitor badges at the Campus security office then guides us around the campus to the Department of Cultural History building. He insists on carrying the document case inside, making it evident that he can't wait to see what we've brought him.

Don unlocks a door and we enter to see a large lab room with bright, overhead lights. He lays the case on one of the long tables and brings gloves for each of us to put on before unpacking the documents, "Body oil deteriorates paper," He warns us.

The first document is carefully removed from its envelope and spread open; Don pulls an overhead magnifier down to study the paper and its ink, taking several full size pictures, as well.

"I'm not an expert in language and would like all of these to be examined by someone much more learned here at the College, that's why I'm taking photos. The signature date is June 6, 1873." He adds and straightens up from peering through the camera.

"This appears to be a partnership agreement in Scottish Gaelic between two men and I think one is named 'Daniel'. The signatures are badly smeared from dampness and I can't read the rest."

Thomas and I look at each other hopefully.

"Let's take a look at the second piece. I'll put this into a flat, acid-free folder rather than its envelope. Better not to refold these, eventually the paper gives out and you get a broken crease which obscures the writing."

He takes the same precautions with the second document and examines it next.

"It appears to be a sale of property and you're right, the coordinates are the same as those on the other. Same dialect, possibly concerning purchase of a granite quarry from some words I recognize. The office at the National Archives of Scotland will need to be queried with the coordinates and possibly the Aberdeen City and Shire archives can help us locate the property. It's a legitimate bill of sale as you can see by the Aberdeen seal placed here," Don points to it before closing up the document.

"Oh, did I mention that one of the sellers is a man named Angus Smith?" He grins with a wide smile.

"Ah ha!" We both say at once and come eagerly around the table to see the actual print on the page.

"Why wouldn't our man Smith have been on the partnership document?" Thomas asks.

"Many things happen in business and partnerships don't always last: death, change in matrimonial status, personality conflicts, shifts in financial status; any one of those can dissolve an agreement," Don concludes.

"There is the possibility that Mr. Smith may have been in the background during the original arrangement or came along later to buy them out. Maybe he gambled and won?" Don laughs.

"We don't know." Thom and I say together, too giddy with the discovery to be serious.

"The date of sale was September 15, 1886. In that time period, many quarrymen were emigrating to the U.S. and other countries where the granite industry was flourishing. Perhaps the work became too demanding; maybe he made his money and wanted out; you may never know," Don says. "I'll do the archives search for you, if you don't mind Sarah, because you've got my curiosity invested now as well."

"What's this last one?" He asks as he takes it out expectantly.

"We think it's some sort of agreement because there are four signatures at the end, but the language is different."

"Let's take a look. It's definitely authentic and appears to be in 1868 but I can't make out the rest of the date." He bends over another section.

"The language is a mix of Gaelic and old German script, the letter 'S' appears as a modern day 'F', etc. Again, I'm unable to interpret the Gaelic but know someone here who can dictate the interpretation. The date is English; looks like it's written by the same person signing it. He straightens up to say "The signature could be from our man Smith again, but it's hard to tell since there's a smudge over most of the name."

"That's disappointing."

"Don't despair, if you're willing to leave this one, we have technology; a "super" microscope that might be able to help us reconstruct the signature."

I look to Thomas. "Let's take advantage of this. We won't get the chance every day."

"I agree, let's leave it." He agrees.

"Fantastic; I'll take personal care of this I swear, and I'll return it to you as soon as possible." Don says.

When our other documents are put between acid-free papers and replaced in the case, we realise the hour is late and we haven't reserved hotel rooms.

"Don, I hate to rush but we need to find rooms for the night and shed the dust of the road," Thomas says. "Can we get together later this evening?"

"Not necessary. There's an open invitation from the wife to bring you two home for the night."

Thom and I both start to protest and don't want to impose, but Donald insists.

"Delores has dinner on the stove and two rooms ready in the 'royal suites', so we won't take 'no' for an answer here folks."

"Well then, I guess that's that. When do we eat?" I recall my last meal was hours ago.

We drop Donald at his car then follow him from the University and over the River Don.

"You didn't mention they'd named a river for you Donnie," I laugh as we meet at his front door.

"Ha-ha, never heard that one before." He gives me a wry look and opens his home to two good friends.

"Delores is charming," I say to Thom as we stand outside on the back deck after a delicious dinner. Lights shine warmly from the Ferguson's home behind us and we watch the sunset together.

"Dee is quite a woman and she puts up with Don," Thomas remarks.

"He's an exuberant sort." I try to put Donnie's large personality as nicely as possible, but have to laugh at my own words.

"He's always been that way and why change perfection," Thomas laughs, too.

"You can see it in their faces; seventeen years together and two kids and they're very happy. I envy them," I tell Thom.

"You do?" He asks.

"Sometimes I feel the waste of the past nine years," I say, feeling a freedom to so that I haven't with anyone else.

"I let Brian's death take me too far away from life," I continue. "We married to spend all our lives together and when it ended the way it did, I let my dreams for the future die with him. After that, I put walls up to prevent it from ever happening again."

"That's understandable," Thom volunteers. "Everyone uses their own timetable for recovery and there's no set schedule; it's just what's in here." He points to my heart.

"Has anyone ever told you you're very wise for such a young guy?" I ask him with a smile as I turn from the sunset to look at him.

"Why no, you're the first," He says and returns my gaze.

I notice his eyes are actually hazel in color; funny I haven't noticed that before, I think.

"Here you two are." Don calls out as he opens the sliding glass door. "Come in here and let's talk genealogy and about what you know so far." We're both actually too road-weary to discuss genealogy at this point, but we dutifully walk toward the door to share all we know with him. It's ten o'clock before we finally turn in.

Don is due at the University at seven thirty so we probably won't see him before leaving. I caught glimpses of the city yesterday on the way in and Aberdeen looks too fantastic to miss. 'Trade you the Stonehaven stop for an Aberdeen tour?' I'd wheedled and he's promised me the 'grande tour'.

When we step outside this morning, the air feels chilly at forty-five degrees.

"Thank heaven you've warmed the car," I say and gather my coat close around me to scramble inside. Soon we're motoring back over the river into the main part of the city whose chimneys and smokestacks look like a scene from a Dickens tale in the morning dampness.

We told Dee we'll return in a couple of hours for our bags and she gave us two places 'you absolutely don't want to miss.' First, we're to stop at a bakery and eat something called a "rowie", also called an Aberdeen Buttery. It's apparently a sort of cross between a cold pancake and croissant, eaten with jam or butter. I have some doubts about the "cold" part but remain willing to try one.

Next, she told us to tour the old home of the Lord Provost, George Skene. It was built in the sixteenth century, and still furnished correct to the period.

Lastly, she recommends we visit St Machar's Cathedral which was first built in 1130 A.D. Her description of its beautiful stained glass windows makes them sound amazing.

"We have a few hours this morning, maybe we should just do a drive-through on Union Street to glimpse all the architecture," I suggest to Thomas.

"I think that would be wise because I have my own ideas on what I'd like to show you." He says mysteriously.

"What is it?" I ask.

"You'll find out, meanwhile I'm keeping it a surprise. We'll make a large circle around Union Street downtown, which will be very busy this morning and should give you plenty of time to goggle like a typical tourist."

"Goggle is it?" I challenge him on his description.

"Yes goggle. Then we'll drive out to the harbor. I think you'll like a place I know there."

"What is it?" I ask again with more emphasis.

"I won't tell." He smiles and I don't ask further.

We turn on Union St. and pass over Denburn Road via the Union bridge. The morning sun peeks from the eastern sky between buildings, and sets off their silvery granite exteriors.

"Wow, it really reminds me of Highbridge, you know?" I remark to Thom.

"That comparison occurred to me on my first visit here. I think now there must be a granite connection and we may find it in the final interpretation of the quarry document," Thom says.

I see we're in the heart of the business district and people are rushing to work, dressed warmly to ward off the morning temperature and the light breeze. As we pass the old Townhouse clock, I notice the time. We really don't have time for a walkabout, so I'm content to sit back and take in as much as possible.

"Of course; there's a McDonald's," I declare upon seeing their familiar colors.

"Why are you surprised?" Thomas asks, "We do have the latest in cuisine to offer to you Americans when you visit."

Next, we drive down to the quays and I see a sign for Footdee Village at the Port. the surprise I'd hinted at.

"Where are we going?" I ask in doubt since the area grows more and more industrial.

"Someplace that used to be a slum a few years ago." Thom answers and I fight down my skepticism.

"Here we are," He announces as we pull in and park on a small street. "Feel like a walk?"

"I'm game if you are," I answer and he opens my car-door.

We walk a brisk pace down the street toward the harbor. There are grey granite houses lining the way, all are renovated with new windows and some with sky-lights on their roofs. When one row ends I look up the narrow street and see several tiny, shed-like cottages in various styles and building materials within the block. All are painted and neat, some with window boxes and obviously from another era; some are two storied, but most sit one story high.

"What are those small buildings?" I ask Thomas.

"This is an ancient fishing village named Footdee which began in the fourteenth century," he says, "we just call it 'Fittie' now. Fishermen and their families lived here and made a good living until the waters were overfished. The land was sold to build the houses any way they liked and each had an outhouse shed, those little cottages you see down the street. In time, the fishermen could no longer make it and moved away. Some emigrated elsewhere and some worked in the granite quarries.

"Eventually oil support vessels for the offshore rigs in the North Sea took over the harbor and brought back income to the city," Thomas finishes.

"Progress can be good and bad can't it," I remark. "I imagine the oil industry has been good for Aberdeen's economy?"

"Yes, especially since the granite industry lost its momentum when other countries, including the U.S., jumped on the bandwagon," Thom says.

I snap pictures of Fittie as we walk and enjoy Thom's history lesson on the area.

We reach the end of the street and stop to read the names on the community monument to the men killed in World War One. I turn to see an unusual restaurant elevated on pilings close by then look out on the harbor.

"Beautiful sunrises from there." Thom remarks as he follows my gaze. "I wish we had time to see one."

"I do too," I agree with him. We walk back to the car as I remember how Thom's eyes studied mine just now.

"I think we have about two hours of time left as tourists," he says. "You'll have to choose between the Provost's house and the Cathedral—your choice."

"Oh, I don't want to miss either one, but in the interest of getting home, I will choose...St Machar's. The Provost house sounds wonderful, but I think it would take more than two hours to digest its contents."

"Good call Sarah, I agree." He turns the car onto King Street toward old Aberdeen and the Chanonry.

The area around the Cathedral Church is near King's College and contains posh housing; grey granite homes their roofs and upper stories visible behind granite walls, sit on the tree-lined street.

A sign posted at the side of the gateway declares its doors open to visitors and we follow the driveway to the Cathedral which sits beyond a venerable graveyard. The memorials and stones, mostly of granite, look to be surviving the centuries well. The genealogist in me longs to walk and read every one of them.

"Look, Thomas, isn't it impressive." I see the silver granite of the building for the first time.

"The towers on the west end were initially built as tower houses." I read from my tablet as he finds a parking place.

"They contained stairs to several floors and were originally topped with small cape houses, until those were replaced with spires later. Look how green everything is, isn't that unusual for late fall?" I take several pictures of the grounds and include a few of the ancient headstones.

"Much of its history is told in its stained glass windows." I put my tablet away and we enter inside.

I walk the entire length of its walls, stopping to study the windows and read inscriptions on the placards below them. Three high windows of stained glass show the Christ, the Last Supper and His Crucifixion along with the Scottish Saints. The windows soar over the altar and the daylight shining through the jewel-like colors casts them down onto the communion table. Small memorial windows line both walls the length of the Church and seven tall windows hold watch over the entry doors we just came through.

"I recall reading that a part of William Wallace's body is rumored to be in these walls, placed here after his execution in 1305," I call to Thom a few steps behind me. I touch my hand to one of the rough, cool granite walls and secretly ask "Are you are here William?"

《 》

I watch as she lays her hand on the wall and looks up at the heraldry on the high wooden ceiling, like some modern Joan of Arc. Sarah is complicated, but it makes her all the more dear to me. I walk to join her as she comes up the center of the aisle, but pauses to take, of all things, a picture of the floor.

"What may I ask are you doing?" I ask her. "All this and you take a picture of the floor?"

She laughs at my tone. "Yes, because this is one of the survivors from the sixteenth century...think of it; this stone I stand on was set in place by a mason somewhere in the fifteen hundreds. Aren't you excited?"

"I forget that you're not exposed to these things on a regular basis as I am." I answer her and admit, "Yes, I should be excited...and was when I first saw it as a young man during my postgraduate tourist trip. What I loved most were the different colors of the stone. It's art, plain and simple, still in existence today and amazing."

She persists. "I'll tell you what impresses me most; in nearly every century this Cathedral was either being built up by its bishops, or destroyed by war or natural disaster. Still, it contains the original nave and its aisles from the 14th and early 15th century. I can't begin to tell you how being here makes me feel Thom. I can sense the presence of those who have given so much in the Church's honor over the centuries; they somehow still watch over and protect these granite walls, I feel certain." Then she suddenly remembers another fact.

"Walls; did you know that the masons who set the stones in the middle ages left their marks on their work and I just saw a couple on the wall back there?" Her face is alight.

I can't help myself and stifle a laugh before saying, "I'm thrilled that you're thrilled Sarah, I really am, but the time is passing by and we need to get back on the road, I'm sorry." I'm aware I've just thrown a wet blanket of sorts on her reverie. She comes back to earth a little too fast and tears well up in her eyes.

"It's beautiful," She whispers.

"Yes, very beautiful." I agree and watch her then open my arms. She steps in to lean on me for comfort and to regain her composure.

"The light is wonderful from these windows." She whispers softly.

"Yes, wonderful," I agree again and enjoy her warmth against me.

"I would need to wear my woolen socks though to attend services; do you feel the cold through your shoes?" She says, and I know the moment has passed.

I release her, "It's the granite floors, resilient, but not too warm. Shall we go?"

"Yes, I'm ready," She says and we slowly walk back up the aisle and outside.

I turn up the car's heat to warm her feet as we ride west, back to Donald's house. Dee comes from the kitchen when we arrive.

"What did you think?" She asks us.

"I loved seeing Aberdeen. Thomas took me down to Footdee."

"Fittie? Did you love it? I've always dreamed of having one of those little houses but we'd never be able to afford one. Besides, the kids would go crazy down there. Where else did you go?" Dee asks.

"We took a street tour of downtown and then stopped at St Machar's; beautiful area and amazing Cathedral... loved its windows," Sarah tells her.

"You did very well for the time at hand. You'll have to come back someday for the full tour."

"I really want to." Sarah says then excuses herself to go upstairs and pack.

« »

Don walks in the front door just as I start upstairs to the do the same.

"Hey mate, how'd you make out on the quick tour this morning?"

"We covered a lot of ground in a short amount of time. Sarah took pictures and mourned the fact that we had to leave. But all in all I think it went as well as you could expect for five hours. What are you doing home at this hour?" I ask him.

"What? I'd let you get away without a send-off, you think? I wanted to talk to you for a minute without the women in earshot; let's take a walk," Don says and leads me to the glass doors outside.

"Okay, but not too far," I tell him, "I'm walked out from this morning."

"Well, old man, do you think you can make it to the deck?" He teases me and we wind up leaning on the far rail to look out on the school practice field behind his house.

"Look here, it's none of my business, but you know me, always intruding where I feel necessary," Don begins. "What's between you and Sarah?"

"What do you mean 'between'?" I ask.

"Don't play coy with me mate; you're in love. It's written all over your face whenever she comes into a room. What have you done about it?"

"Do we have to talk about this now?" I fire back.

"Yes, now; you want to wait till we see you again in five years? Spill it," Don demands.

"Alright...here it is. Yes, I'm in love with her. I kissed her twice in one evening when we'd both had a little to drink. I apologized the next morning and things have been normal between us since then. There, are you happy?"

"Happy? Heck no, I'm not happy. Look here," Don calms himself and lowers his voice, "this is the first person you've genuinely fallen for since that little exercise in your twenties; how is Lydia by the way, don't answer that now. You're not going to let Sarah get away are you?"

"Are you quite finished?" I ask.

"Yes," He says and looks me in the eye then leans against the rail to wait on my answer.

"She's just come out of her grief for Brian after nine years. I don't want to rush her into something she's not ready for."

"Did she tell you not to rush her?" Don questions.

"Well, no but she talked about 'building walls' and not letting anyone in. I took that to mean that she's still not ready."

He takes pity on an old friend and throws an arm over my shoulders. "Look mate, she's ready, she just doesn't realise it. You've got to make her see she's ready."

"But how do I do that? I'm on new ground here," I run a hand over my hair, "If I rush her she may bolt back to the U.S. and I'll never see her again. If I don't rush her, she may leave right on schedule, which by the way is in another week and I'll never see her again. Quite a choice if you ask me."

"I feel your pain Thom, but just remember this. It will be easier to woo her while she's here than when she's five thousand miles away."

"Understood..." I tell him, "I'll think of something."

"Good. And how is Lydia?" Don asks.

"She's well and loving life." At that moment, Dee opens the door and calls us in for lunch.

"Thanks for the prep talk, Don. I might have known you were up for the job."

"You got it mate, anytime, you know that."

« »

We've been on the road about an hour and a half, almost to Perth, so I decide to open up the basket that Dee repacked and sent with us.

"Oh my, Dee may have surpassed our Jamie when it comes to road trip provisions," I tell Thomas.

"Why?" He asks.

"Well, if I'm not mistaken, these match the description of butteries that we didn't have time to sample. She's a baker now isn't she, do you suppose she made these just for us?"

"Wouldn't put it past her, what else is in there?" He glances over as I investigate.

"Cold chicken salad, what looks like some sort of hot soup in a thermos, fresh baked oatmeal bread and several little cakes in different flavors. Remind me to have her cater the next affair my mother throws, we can order ahead by mail." I laugh in delight then stop.

"What's wrong?" Thomas asks.

"I forgot my parents won't be around when I get back. I'm not sure how I feel about that," I say a little shaky.

"I'm sorry." He reaches for my hand, "I know you're close."

"It's strange isn't it? They've been nearby since the day I was born. During the last fourteen years, I married, became widowed and worked at a living, just in the next town from them. The difference now is knowing they're inaccessible except by phone; a psychological thing I guess." I look down at his hand over mine.

"I know you'll do fine Sarah, in the meantime, you plan to return to Florida pretty soon, right?" He asks.

"Yes, I think I've gone as far as I can on the groundwork, it's up to Donnie to get back with results of his inquiries on the land location and the other documents. When he does, I hope you'll write or give me a call so that I can keep up to date?"

"Of course I will; no need to worry there," He says.

"Good." I turn my attention back to the basket; "Now, what can I feed you while you're driving?"

"Give me one of those butteries things, I've never had one," He grins at me.

"You're kidding, right? You're born and raised in the U.K.; didn't these things travel down to the Estate?"

"Nope, not even a crumb. I really wonder just when they were invented, I can't remember them as a young man and I occasionally traveled on import business to Aberdeen. Could it be a tourist gimmick?" He asks.

"If it is," I swallow a quick bite, "they have us; this is good."

We make excellent time down through Edinburgh and the Northumberland National Park. The light remains sufficient for a couple of pictures at Hadrian's Wall... albeit quickly, I jump out, take them and jump back into the car.

By the time we drive up to Highbridge, it is eight p.m. and we wearily pull ourselves out of the car. Thomas brings our bags inside the back door just as Emily and Stephen are finishing up their late dinner.

"Well, welcome home son." Stephen gives him a big hug, "And you, too," he gives me the same.

"Were you able to put up with my son for two days in a row?" Stephen asks.

"Yes, no problems and we have no bruises to show for it either," I answer him.

"Well come in and sit down, or stand as you wish" he adds as he sees both of us cringe when the word 'sit' is mentioned.

"Dad, I can't speak for Sarah, but I need to freshen up and change clothes.

"I just want to steam in the shower for a while," I reply.

"How about we both meet you in the great room in say an hour and I promise we'll catch you up to speed on the trip?" Thomas suggests.

"Splendid plan; you two go on and I'll see you later." Stephen agrees.

When I reach my room, Tom is asleep outside the door.

"Well, well old fella, what have you been up to in my absence, eh?" He circles my legs as I open the door then goes directly to his feed dish in the bathroom.

"Ok, I can see nothing has changed here," I call to him as his tail disappears around the doorframe.

I pull out some loungewear from the closet and go directly to the shower. An hour later I feel much more human.

Tom runs out the door when I open it and heads for the back stairs; I turn to the front stairs down to the great room. Looking over the rail I see Berty bring in a tray of something and put it on the table. "Berty, how are you?"

He turns and smiles as I come down the stairs. "Very good, Miss Sarah; I hope your trip proved useful?"

"Yes, it did and we may have found new information on Stephen's great grandfather, but please don't tell him as you're the first to hear it at Highbridge."

He looks pleased and makes a motion to zip his lips. "Mums the word Miss." He turns back toward the kitchen.

"What was that all about?" Thomas asks as he walks from the stairs.

"I just told Berty a little about our findings with Don and made him promise not to tell your father until we told him first."

"Berty is very good at keeping secrets," Thomas says, "I'm sure there'll be no problem, however, you've no doubt made a friend for life."

« »

I survey my road trip partner and see a beautiful, slightly weary woman with tendrils of auburn hair around her face. I unconsciously reach for one and put it behind her ear.

"I see you've just come from the shower," I tell her.

She seems somewhat shaken by my touch. "Yes, I didn't have energy to do anything with it," She replies.

"It's okay," I smile at her. "I like it this way."

"You do? A girl could save a lot on salon time with someone like you," she tells me.

Our eyes hold for a few seconds.

217

"Alright you two." Stephen calls as he enters the room, "Come over here and tell me all. How did your trip go?" We take a seat on the couch opposite him.

"It was a good trip, there were so many things to see and experience," Sarah happily answers.

"Yes, Sarah packed in as much sight-seeing as possible this morning." I add, "Don and his wife Dee provided us rooms for the night in their home and they couldn't have been more hospitable."

"It's good to have friends you can depend upon. Glad to hear Don is happy and well. I remember him coming home with you a few times during breaks from university, quite a nice chap indeed." Stephen says, "So tell me about his thoughts on the documents you took up."

"Does the name Angus Smith mean anything to you Dad?"

"Angus Smith." Stephen wrinkles his brows and remains silent for a few moments. "Can't say as it does, should it?"

"He sold the land in the document and the coordinates on the land matched those mentioned in the other agreement," Sarah says.

"Intriguing to be sure but unfortunately I've never heard the name before; my father never mentioned it either."

"Don seems to think the coordinates may have something to do with a granite quarry." Sarah quickly adds.

"Yes, he offered to research the land location and anything else he can find in the Aberdeen archives," I tell him. "He's retained one document and will use some of their high tech equipment to reconstruct the signature that's smudged." Dad seems impressed.

"In the meantime Stephen," Sarah speaks up, "we need to reexamine any documents here, including the plans for the house and receipts for materials, especially those for any of the granite."

"Right, good thinking, Sarah. And did you enjoy the countryside, Aberdeen met your expectations?" Dad asks.

"Oh, I had a wonderful time. Thomas made the perfect tour guide for the City and on the road. I took lots of pictures and will try to get them onto a disc so that we can watch them before I return to the States next week."

"Next week? That soon, eh," Dad remarks, "It seems your time here has absolutely flown my dear. And what a great job you've done for us too. We would never have gotten this far without your insights and work."

"I've had the most fun Stephen; it didn't seem like work at all," She says.

"Well, I know you both must be road weary. Emily sent some food for you if you're interested; it's over there on the tray. I've already eaten so I will say good night and see you in the morning."

« »

Stephen walks upstairs and I get up from the couch to see what the tray holds; "Hot corned beef and Swiss sandwiches, they look pretty good and are still warm, want one?"

"I could eat a little; come join me." Thomas picks up one of the sandwiches and comes to sit by the fire. "When will you be off to Florida?" He asks.

"I called last week and booked a week from Thursday. That should give me time to document the results of the research and wrap things up here. I have to get Tom used to his carrier again, and I'm sure it will take some readjustment for him to be without Missy."

"And you? What are your plans after your return Sarah?" Thomas puts the remains of his sandwich back on the tray.

"I think I'll be readjusting as well." I rise and poke at one of the burning logs with the fireplace iron. "You've...all become very dear to me...right down to Emily, Megg and even Berty. But this..." I wave an arm over the room as I walk to him, "It's the stuff of dreams in a little girl's head. It's been almost surreal for me, Thomas and I need to go home and deal with the reality of my world. Do you understand?" I place a hand fondly on his face and hold it there as he places his over it.

220

"I understand it Sarah...not because I want to, but because I must. You've made up your mind and if I've learned anything in the past five weeks, it's that you stick to your decisions." Then he takes my hand to his chest and rests it over his heart.

"Just promise me to keep in contact after you go back?" he says quietly, "Don't leave me wondering what you're about; Promise me Sarah?"

"I promise." I say and mean it.

<< >>

This week I've completed a suggested pedigree chart of Thomas' newly discovered ancestors and a timeline graph using the dates on the documents, forward through Charles, Stephen and Thomas' life events.

Strange this doesn't add up yet though. There would almost have to be another generation level for this to work. It's a letdown to realise that despite all our discoveries, there's still so much more to find. The last information I've added is Highbridge's construction date in 1887, thanks to the drawings we found in the secret bookcase.

There's blank space on the graph awaiting results of Donald's research in the Aberdeen archives and Ted's findings on the New Zealand Cross awardees. I hope to find something online which brings forth birth and death dates for the Angus Smith of the sales agreement and I will search from home for details of Thomas' great grandfather's life, including military draft registration, war record, pension records, wills and where he lived upon discharge.

I've been at genealogy long enough to know things aren't always as they appear or as you want them to be. If more documented proof on Angus isn't found we'll be unable to prove the relationship to Stephen.

I get up stiffly from my computer and walk to the window. The sun has decided to show brightly this afternoon and the blue sky outlines the tree-line above the house. All of it calls to me but I must choose to stay in the library to finish up and print out copies for Thomas and his father before leaving tomorrow.

The graphs and the "suggested" lineage from Angus are finally burned on discs and I close the files with a finality that gives me satisfaction, but some sadness. I look at the beautiful library, my workspace for many weeks and whisper 'I will miss you old friend' then pick up my briefcase and walk away.

Everyone has come to dinner this evening, even Berty and Emily are with us at the kitchen table and Jamie joins us when all is ready. Stephen suggested the dining room in honor of my last night, but I insisted the kitchen would be the most comfortable and I'd like to think of them there after returning home.

"Then here's a toast." Stephen rises from his chair. "To Sarah, who's stirred up more excitement around here than we've seen in many a year. We send with you our heartfelt wishes for your health and success in whatever you pursue in future."

I thank him for his generous toast and stand to make one of my own.

"I'm not as good at this as Stephen, but I'm willing to try." I look around the table at them all.

"I think Paul Theroux said it best, 'A tourist doesn't know where he's been, a traveler doesn't know where he's going.' You see, the tourist is me when I first came to Highbridge. Because of your generosity and spirit, I've graduated from tourist to traveler, someone who can leave home and feel comfortable wherever they are. I don't know where I'm going in life, but I have you all to thank for my new confidence to face the world and not just exist in my little home town in Florida. Thank-you so much, I love you all." I lift my glass to each person at the table, beginning with Thomas.

Chapter 8 Epiphany

My last evening around the big kitchen table at Highbridge is frequently on my mind.

It's been a week since I left with everyone waving goodbye to me from the front steps. Berty drove me down to Manchester Airport; Thomas couldn't accompany us due to a last minute meeting scheduled for the mill. I am surprised by the feelings his absence raised in me, but once I arrived at my front door and stepped inside, I felt better.

Tom bucked up after his brief period of separation anxiety from Missy and has returned to his old eating habits.

My parents are busy being "island people" as Dad calls it and invited me down for a vacation. I told them 'not yet, I've just come home' and they understand.

I tell myself that boredom follows a fairy tale experience such as the one I've just finished, but after a week home I realise my boredom is extreme and finally own up to it. This morning, I decide to channel my restlessness into something useful, a certification in genealogy.

Online I'm intrigued with an association specializing in British Isles research, which links to several other online courses. I begin with the basics just to make sure I fill any gaps in my existing experience over the years then add new courses to bring myself up to speed on resources in the U.K. and Scotland.

A month later as I sit at the computer reviewing what I've learned, I'm amazed what one can do to change one's life by just taking a first step.

The doorbell interrupts my reflections and I find a package left on the step then wave to the postman as he pulls away.

I note with surprise the box is from the U.K. and go to the kitchen for my favourite paring knife/box cutter. Inside the box I find a framed picture I'd forgotten about. Stephen bought a new camera during my visit and wanted to try it out, so he called me and Thomas outside from the library. It was a sunny day, we were in good spirits and we hammed it up on the front terrace for him.

My knees suddenly go weak and I sit down heavily at the breakfast bar.

Happy! It hits me out of the blue. I was happy in Highbridge, doing what I liked with people I admired...and loved.

"With Thomas." I say it out loud and repeat it again. "I was happy with Thomas." My epiphany is complete.

I look back at the picture and admire his clean cut Brit chin, his smiling eyes and his dark hair that's always falling down his forehead. I remember his efforts to make me admit even a little that I cared for him; how he held my hand when I talked about Brian's death; and how he was always so considerate of me whether it was an umbrella in the rain or warmth in the car for a drive so I wouldn't be chilled.

I remember his kisses, the first one in the great room that I chalked up to the brandy and wine; how crass of me. His second at my door when his touch put butterflies in my stomach. But some stubbornness inside me prevented any response to him, despite the fact I was drawn to him.

"I am an idiot!" I say out loud to the empty house. Tom comes from his perch on the bed to stroke against my leg. When I don't pay attention to him, he stands up and puts both paws on my lap and stares at me until I absent-mindedly begin to pet him. Then I look at him.

"It's ok my friend, I know what to do; it's time." He stands down again, licks a paw and retires back to the bedroom for a midmorning nap.

I'm going to the nearest real estate broker in the morning, I think. This house belonged to Brian and me but that life is fading away. It's as if a weight holding me down for nine years has lifted. There's no guilt; somehow I know Brian is okay with it.

Strangely, within a week a buyer appears, offers cash with a deposit and plans are made to close on the first of December.

I call my parents and spend an hour on the line with them discussing Thomas and his family. I relate how I've come to recognise my love for him and they're surprised because I barely mentioned him during our conversations overseas. Recognising the love in my voice, they express how happy they are for me.

My next call is to Stephen's private number and he answers on the second ring.

"Please don't say more if Thomas is there with you." I warn him.

"That is the case." He says.

"Hello Stephen, it's Sarah. I'm calling because I realise ...I'm in love with your son."

"That's wonderful, I'm glad the book came in," He declares.

"It took me a while, but it all became apparent after I received the picture you took of us. You sent it for a reason didn't you."

"Yes that's right." He bluffs for Thomas' benefit.

"I need to talk with you in confidence Stephen; if you call me later when you're alone, I would so appreciate it. I have a plan and hope that you can help me."

« »

"Of course, of course. I'll let you know as soon as possible," I say to Sarah, "good bye." I hang up and cast a sideways glance over to Thomas.

"Who was that Dad?" He asks.

228

"Oh...ah...the bookstore in York," I invent in the moment. "I ordered something on old mills and they have one in, wanted to know if I'd pick it up."

I smile as I think of what might follow with these young people and start to whistle my favourite bridge tune. Thomas looks up at me with curiosity but then returns to his work.

《 》

Later in the evening, my phone rings. I push Tom off my lap and rush to pick it up.

"Sarah!" Stephen's voice booms. "I say; good news this morning."

"Don't tell Thomas any of what we talk about, Stephen; I want to tell him in person. I owe him that after the way I ignored his affection, promise?" I ask.

"I promise, Sarah. Now what can I do to help?"

"Here's the plan. I'm coming back over there and I'll need a small cottage to call my own. Can you recommend a realtor who can be trusted?"

"Yes, of course, but why not stay here, you know we have plenty of room," Stephen asks.

"I know, but I don't want to work Thomas into a corner in case he has doubts or needs to take some time. And just maybe Stephen, we both need more time, a lot happened during my five week stay."

"You're right of course my dear and both of you deserve time to get it right. I'll email you with the name of an estate agent tomorrow. Now, what's next?" Stephen says in excitement.

"I'd like to use the research we conducted on your family line as a write-up for my application to the genealogy society, but I want to work in research for a couple of years over there for the experience before certification. Would you have any problem with my sharing your story?" I ask hopefully.

"Why no, I don't believe so. Nothing there that I'm ashamed of and if it will help you, please go ahead," Stephen says.

"Thank you Stephen, this is all falling into place so wonderfully. I've sold my house it closes the first of December." I plunge on, "I want to have my parents up to the U.K. for Christmas time at my cottage. It would be nice to get our two families acquainted don't you think?"

"Capital idea, Sarah! I'm going to whip up the best Christmas this old house has seen in many years. Now you leave all the rest to me. By the way, can I at least let Megg in on the surprise? She's very trustworthy and could be invaluable as a helper for you without raising suspicion when I'm unable to get away."

"That's a great idea Stephen, please do so, I know she can be trusted, look at the great job she did for you at the company for so long."

I hang up, very excited about the plan. The thing I'm guilty about is not sharing my feelings right away with Thomas, so I decide to call him...just to check in as I promised to do.

I ring him up on his cell and hear his familiar voice answer on the other end.

"Sarah, how are you? It's been more than a month," he scolds me. "I've missed you."

"That's sweet Thomas, I've missed all of you too," but I know he hadn't meant it in that way.

"Guess what I've been doing?" I challenge him.

"Can't imagine." He replies rather dryly.

"I'm working on a certification in genealogy."

"That's wonderful; I know how you love it, Sarah and you are very good at it."

"Thank-you Thomas, the great thing is I can actually offer my services for document research and make a reasonable living doing what I enjoy."

"That's good Sarah, I'm glad you're finding your direction."

He doesn't know the half of it, I think. "So what have you heard from Don or Ted; anything?"

"No, nothing yet," He replies. "I spoke with Don yesterday and he's filed a query with the Archives but received no reply. I'm afraid it's a rather slow business."

"And how is the mill coming along; any idea for a completion date?"

"We're going for completion next May, provided the weather isn't too uncooperative this winter. Concrete doesn't set at very low temperatures so I'm praying for a mild winter. If not, it will be mid-summer."

"And is everyone in good health there?"

"Yes, very well. Sarah, what are your plans for Christmas?"

"Well...I'm going to see my parents in St Thomas." I don't feel good saying it.

"Oh." His despondent reply hurts me and I consider telling him the truth, but fight it down.

"Thomas, please be patient with me...I do miss you."

"Of course, you have my word, Sarah."

When we hang up, I feel we've connected over those words and that Thomas might at least feel a little better.

I've called the Estate agent whom Stephen recommended.

"Mr. Tolar, good afternoon, this is Sarah Sandlin in the U.S."

"Oh Miss Sandlin, yes, Mr. Smith said you'd call. He filled me in on the situation and I think I might just have what you're looking for."

"Really, how wonderful. I'm anxious to hear about it."

"It's a new listing just on the market. A small cottage, not far out of the Village; two bedrooms, two baths, sits on its own land, has a garden too if you're interested in that sort of thing."

"I'm surprised at the second bath Mr. Tolar, how did that happen?"

"Well, the person who owned the place had planned to rent it via a holiday rental agency, until she unexpectedly passed away and the family is interested to get it off their hands, so to speak. Shall I send you some pictures and a map of the location?"

"Yes, please. What price range are we in?"

"It's at £167,000, that's about $280,591 US."

"That would be perfect, of course depending upon its condition and working order. This would be a cash transaction Mr. Tolar."

"Oh I think you'll find everything up to standard, but we'll deal with that after you see the info. I'll send it with pictures to your email right away."

"Thank-you sir, I look forward to it."

The pictures come through within the hour and I enter the address to a satellite search to see the terrain. I zoom in on its location at the other side of the Village and there doesn't seem to be a flood plain, but I'll check the government website just to make sure.

All in all, a nice little piece of property I think and send back a few questions regarding the septic system, the roof and the plumbing. I decide to let Mr. Tolar know that Stephen will look over the property as my representative, but send back some of my questions; is this an outright sale as a freehold or will it come under a leasehold interest, that sort of thing.

Boredom is no longer an issue with me. I have more than enough activity in getting ready for this rather sudden move.

I walk through the house with new eyes and see a few things I need to ship to the U.K., but I'd best travel light I think; they have flea markets there as well and it will be fun to pick up bargains again. I feel certain Stephen won't mind lending me some of his attic treasures in the meantime.

I wonder if my buyer would like to receive this house furnished? The realtor returns my call within the hour to say he's talked with the buyers; they are interested in the furniture and want to know how much it will add to the price. My answer comes easy: "Not a penny, just take good care of it."

I talk once more to Stephen after he's taken a walk-thru of the cottage.

"It's quite a steal, Sarah and a good choice by Mr. Tolar. The septic system, roof and pipes have recently been redone and are under guarantee. As he said, the previous owner planned to open it as a B&B. The heat is oil-powered boiler and radiators in all rooms, with a cozy gas fireplace in the lounge. There's even a small detached shed big enough for one car in the back which is a real bonus in our weather."

"What do you think, Stephen?" I ask him. "Please give me your honest opinion, is it a good price and do you see any problems that could spring up?"

"I think it's in very good shape for being sixty years old and I believe you'll like it. It just needs your special touch to make it home," He adds.

"Now Sarah, something occurred to me last night. I have questions about your status in the country as a resident; have you taken care of any issues regarding your visa?"

"Stephen, I just explored that today and before you say it, yes, I know it was stupid of me to wait so long. I find that I will need an employment position lined up before a visa will be approved and I don't know where to go from here."

"I think I can solve that and offer you a permanent position as our family's genealogy researcher at an adequate salary. Let me look into the specifics and I'll get back to you in a day or so. Don't worry Sarah, we'll get this taken care of." He hangs up before I have time to protest or to thank him.

I look around my little house this morning. After a cleaning rampage yesterday, I threw out things that I no longer need. The trash man will have a fit when he sees the curb this morning. Over by the doorway a pile of boxes sit taped and labeled in a stack, ready for shipping. Tom lays upon the uppermost box as if to say, 'when are we leaving?'

I give him a good pet. "Don't worry fella; no way would I leave you here." The phone rings and Stephen greets me in his usual large way.

"Hello my dear, how are you today? I just left my solicitor's office and he assures me that hiring you for the job will go a long way to having the visa approved. He is going to take care of the particulars and will be sending you some papers to fill out and sign. Get them back to him overnite and he'll take care of the rest." He pauses to catch his breath and I jump in.

"Stephen, slow down. This will cost you money for the attorney; please tell me his fee so that I can send him a cheque."

"My dear, he's on permanent retainer with me, so that is not an issue. If you wish, you may send the proper fee amount for the visa when we know more. For now, it is taken care of, no further argument expected."

"How will I ever repay you for all your help these past few weeks?"

"Consider it done. I have no daughters and you are daily coming closer to filling that gap. Thomas told me he has heard from you, said you missed him. Most humane thing you could do to put him out of his misery and that's what he's been since you left—miserable." He chuckles in sympathy for the boy.

"Thank you Stephen."

"We'll talk again." And so we have, for what seems hundreds of minutes until at last, all is taken care of that either of us can think of.

I have an invisible list in my head which I periodically search through and check for things I may have missed: The application has been filed for a work visa after necessary papers for the job were signed; Tom is "legal", all his papers, his microchip, his forms, etc. will be with me. The estate agent organised some small repairs at the cottage and I signed and sent the completion documents via overnight mail to Stephen who's attending the final meeting.

All my packages have been picked up and shipped, to be delivered to the cottage the day after I arrive on December 14th; my parents will arrive at Manchester December 22nd just in time for shopping and Christmas festivities.

And lastly, Meggs offered to pick me up since I still don't trust myself to drive any sort of vehicle on the left side of the highway.

It's my last night home and I sit here in my favorite chair thinking about Highbridge and the week to come. First to Atlanta then to London Heathrow with Tom and everything I still own, which isn't much at this point. Albums, genealogy files and a few mementos from my earlier school years are packed. Another small box contains a few things important from life with Brian, to be opened in years to come should there be a need. All my clothes except for those in my carry-on have been shipped.

Important papers are with me; birth certificate, diplomas, visa, passport, my laptop and a survival kit for Tom until we reach our new home in the village.

Enough; no more reviewing 'the list' I think. I look at the once-welcoming house, now empty of everything I've accumulated in the last ten years, except furniture.

I feel the moment's melancholia in my heart; this is hard, but it's unthinkable that I could be happy without Thomas.

« »

I drive my car through the Village on the way to Sarah's new house. Looks very festive today on Main Street and I admire the shops with their decorations on full display. Every merchant has lights around their windows and doors and the Council has coordinated some light strings across the street in front of the war memorial as well. This is my new home, too, now that I'm part of Highbridge and I'm growing to love it.

I turn right at the lane on the other side of the Village and follow the fence line for a half-mile until the little cottage comes into sight then pull the car around back to park.

Gathering my notebook along with my bag, I walk to the kitchen door, but look across the fields for a moment to watch some sheep as they graze on the side of the hill. This will make a nice view in the summer when Sarah sits outside I think as the new key turns perfectly in the door lock.

I put my things down on the kitchen table which, along with some other furniture was brought over from Highbridge's attic storage last week by John. I cautioned him that 'this is our little secret' and he made me smile when he remarked 'what furniture Megg?' I promised him it would all make sense very soon.

The cleaning lady has spruced up the cooker and fridge and put a sheen on the floor. *Good, it needed it* I think. I hang a couple of dish towels beside the sink and stand back to see that they look quite fresh with their red checkered pattern.

Walking through the little hallway past the stairway, I see all is in order in the lounge. The couch and side chairs have been cleaned and are spotless. I drape a cozy throw over the side of the couch; nights can sometimes get drafty.

The past week has been a busy one getting the cottage in order, cleaned and furnished. I wanted it to be ready for the holidays and brought in a few things from my old

London apartment, including Christmas decorations for the mantel and the rooms upstairs.

I climb the narrow stairway to the two small bedrooms next. Both rooms have brand new queen-sized mattresses which Sarah asked that I purchase. Thick rugs for each bedroom and bath, enough linen to last a couple of weeks through the holidays and toiletries for the baths have been provided.

"Perfect." I say aloud with a satisfied smile as I walk back down the staircase to the kitchen and take one last look before returning to Highbridge. What a charming little cottage. It reminds me so much of the one my husband and I first started out in. Life was happy for us in London and it's a nice memory, but Douglas has been gone almost 21 years. Now that I'm older I do miss the companionship and shared experiences that marriage holds. Ah well, a bit late for all that now and besides, I'm happier than I've been in a long time thanks to Stephen's generosity.

I glance at the little clock on the mantle and realise I'd best get back before someone starts looking for me. It's been difficult "sneaking around" as Stephen calls it, so that Thomas and the rest of the household don't catch on to Sarah's return. Helping with the "plan" has certainly raised my spirits for the season, a good thing since I'm working with Emily on the Christmas Eve celebration.

Stephen has invited friends of Thomas' from Aberdeen with their teenagers, and families from the Village. Knowing how he adores children, I'm sure he'll do something special to entertain them. How different it is now that we're both out of the business setting and have a chance to get better acquainted. He's truly a good man and his friendship means a great deal to me.

«»

At the closing, the elderly couple thank me, saying it is the nicest thing anyone had ever done for them and a real surprise to include furniture at no cost. I tell them it was easy and proves that furniture does not a home make. It's what a person brings of self that opens up a house, making it a place where people want to be. Take that away and all that's left is wood, wiring and plumbing.

I leave Mom and Dad's house this morning by taxi; thank heavens I still have a key to their house since the buyers took possession of my house right after closing. I've already said my goodbyes to life here and it's with a mix of melancholia and excitement that I watch the familiar streets and landmarks fall away behind me.

One thing for sure, after getting comfortably seated on my connecting flight in Atlanta, the accumulated exhaustion of the last few weeks descends upon me. The plane leaves the runway and I rest my head on the back of the seat.

I awake and sit up straighter to look out the window. Nothing like sleeping through your entire trip I think and at that moment the pilot announces we will be setting down shortly. I see a light snow on the approaching tarmac and can't help but smile in anticipation; I'm coming in for a landing.

Debarkation is slow as everyone makes their way off with carry-ons into the passport control area. I present my passport, a copy of my visa and the legal papers for the position with Stephen. His solicitor advised I carry everything with me and I'm glad as the officials are deadly serious in their work. After they check their computers I am cleared for entry, warned not to change address without notification to the local Immigration office.

Next, the Customs officer does a thorough baggage search while I think about Tom in his carrier on a separate path from me. His microchip will be checked against his vet's paperwork and queried electronically before approval. I'd been warned it could take 1-2 hours, but hope it will take less since today is a weekday.

Thank heavens for Stephen and his solicitor I think as I wheel my bag to the passenger pickup area. What a relief to find Megg already here and waving at me.

"Oh Megg, it's so good to see you!"

"Wonderful to see you too, Sarah," she says as we share a quick hug then put the luggage in the trunk and jump into the car without creating too much delay in the pickup lanes.

"I thought I would never get through Customs."

"Did they give you much trouble?" She asks.

"It did seem harder than just being a tourist on holiday and of course, this is my second trip in a short amount of time. Thank heaven they found my visa application in the computer and that I had all my documents. I'm just so glad that's over with."

Megg expertly finds the separate freight terminal where we will pick up Tom. She parks while I run inside the building. Tom is already cleared by Customs and after bringing his carrier to the back seat, we're off. The morning traffic has cleared so we merge easily onto the motorway east.

At the cottage, we park in the back and retrieve Tom and the luggage. I pause to look out across the fields and drink in the peaceful country scene.

"It's truly beautiful; I can't believe my luck in finding this place." I wheel Tom up to the kitchen door and walk in behind Megg.

"Oh my." I see the little kitchen table with its cloth and container of flowers in its centre and the red-checkered towels at the sink.

"You've made this so welcoming." I hug my friend.

"Well," Megg says as she swipes at a tear, "couldn't just throw you in here and wish you luck, now could we?"

I remove my coat and scarf then take Tom out of his carrier, giving him some water after the long trip.

"Give me the tour Megg." She leads the way into the lounge then upstairs to the bedrooms. I can't believe how much work has gone into the furnishings and the small personal touches.

"Megg, you've done too much, I don't know how you've handled all this in such a short time."

"Now, you know I managed an entire company of men for many years don't you? Unbelievable how many hats I had to wear just to keep that company's board on the right path." She laughs, "Compared to that, this was 'a piece of cake.'"

"I know it wasn't quite that easy, but you'll never admit it. Just know that my heart is forever grateful."

"Well, you're welcome, Sarah; if there's nothing you need, I'd best get back to Highbridge before I'm missed too much. So far the "sneaking around" has gone well and it would be a shame to ruin it at this late date. By the way, I took the liberty of picking up a few groceries for you, since you have no car."

"Wonderful. Thank you Megg."

"And the gas is on so you can have a fire tonight if you wish. The thermostats are on the radiators in each room, that's where you control the heat. If you have any other questions just call me, no matter what time and I will answer."

Before she goes out the kitchen door, she turns to ask, "When do your parents come in?"

"They'll be at Manchester next week on the 22nd, but you don't have to worry about them. Dad will rent a car and feels very confident on the left side of the road now that they've been in St Thomas a few months."

"Oh good, but if you need anything before they get here, please call me."

"I will Megg; thanks again and please pass my thanks along to Stephen as well when you see him."

I watch her drive out the lane then go inside to survey my new home. I decide to light the gas fireplace after all and am delighted there is no problem.

Tom has explored every nook and cranny for the past hour and is now upstairs on one of the new beds.

I take my bags up to unpack and use the chest of drawers in the east bedroom as my own. The closets are small, but adequate; the baths are quite nice and even have heated towel racks. Each bedroom has an end window as well as an eyebrow window on the front of the house, which makes them well lighted, even in late afternoon.

I know Megg has outdone herself when I see a feather comforter on each bed and the small touches in the baths, right down to some bath salts that I know my mother will enjoy.

Finished unpacking, I take my bags downstairs to the back door to store in the car shed later.

The kitchen cupboards and fridge are fully stocked; I see microwave meals, breakfast cereals, bread and sandwich supplies, soups, peanut butter, jam and Tom's food. That Megg, she's thought of everything.

I take my supper of soup and crackers to the lounge to watch the fire and deescalate after the day's activities. A few hours ago I was on another continent; this is comfortable, but doesn't feel "normal" yet and I expect it may be several weeks before it does.

Tom wanders down from upstairs and stretches out before the fire.

"You don't seem to have any trouble adjusting." He looks at me, gives a big yawn and falls back asleep.

I watch the flames for a while then take my empty bowl to the kitchen sink. The shipped boxes should be here tomorrow, better get some rest and be ready in case they arrive early. The fireplace and lights are turned off and I climb the stairs to bed, with Tom right behind me.

I awake to the sound of a large vehicle working its way up the lane and bounce out of bed to peer through the window at the new day.

"The delivery truck, oh no!" I hurry to throw on some jeans and a sweatshirt and lock Tom in the bathroom then bound downstairs just in time to open the front door as the driver walks up to knock.

"Good morning Miss, got some boxes here, where would you like 'em?"

"Oh just over here I think." I point to the corner of the front room.

The driver pauses, "You're American aren't you?"

"Yes," I smile, "but I'm becoming more Brit each day."

《 》

I find Dad at his desk when I walk into the construction shed this morning. When he sees me he starts to rearrange his papers.

"Good morning son, how are you?"

"I'm well Dad, how are you?" I'm rather puzzled at his harried demeanor.

"I'm good." he booms. "Finalized some plans for the holiday party."

"Good, I think it's going to be fine." I hang up my coat on the way to my desk. "We'll see the first floor of the Mill finished this morning, that's cause for celebration."

"Absolutely." Dad agrees.

"I think at the end of the day we'll break until after the holidays," I continue. "All the men have plans and places to be with their families, so we'll start our holiday tomorrow. That leaves me with time on my hands; what can I do to help with the party?"

"Well, Thomas I do need a few things taken care of for the children."

"Fire away Dad."

247

"I need a bloke to play Father Christmas; any suggestions?"

"Well, if you have the costume, how about Jamie?" I laughingly suggest.

"Oh no - no, that would never work, he's over his head in providing all the food."

"Alright, I'll work on it, maybe someone from outside the house? I'll let you know by tomorrow. What else?"

"We need some gifts taken care of, electronics for Donald's children and some toys for our little guests as well as their parents, that sort of thing. Do you think you can handle it?"

"Well, yes, but it would be easier if you loan me Megg. Gifts for ladies are not one of my strengths."

"Oh right you are, good idea. Get with her and plan an outing as soon as possible and get everything wrapped when you buy it. No use wasting precious time by doing it ourselves. Have it delivered, so you don't have to carry packages."

"No problem Dad. What else?"

"I've ordered a tree and it comes tomorrow. And I've asked Berty and Emily to be in charge and get John's two young men in to help move furniture in the great room," Dad continues with relish. "Ask if she needs anything for the tree, it's been a long time since we did this. Maybe go up in the attic and see if any decorations are left up there that we can use? I think that's quite enough for your plate son, don't you? If you do finish ahead of time, check back with me and I'll give you some more."

Dad continues with work on his desk, but I take the list from our conversation and drive up to the house to find Emily in the great room with Megg.

"I've already gone to the attic," Emily informs me, "and we have plenty of decorations, but no lights for a large tree. So please put those on your list if you don't mind, Mr. Thomas."

"Will do; now Megg, can we get together tomorrow to go into York and raid their stores?"

"Oh goodness," she hesitates for she knows she should check on Sarah, "how about ten o'clock sir?"

"That sounds good, Meggs. Come round the back and I'll have the car warmed up ahead of time. See you ladies later at dinner." I wave and walk off to my room to think of who would make a good Father Christmas.

《 》

Megg knocks on my kitchen door early this morning and I've just put on the coffee.

"Megg, come in it's cold, you're already out and about? How about some coffee?"

"Thanks but I can't stay, just a check to see if you need anything and if you're doing ok. I'm so sorry to come at this time, but Stephen's got Thomas and me in York for gift buying today and of course, Thomas wants to leave at ten a.m. I'm by here early so he won't wonder what I'm about." She pauses for a breath.

"That's quite alright, I was already awake," I reassure her. "And in answer to your question, no, I don't need a thing, you've already seen to it all. By the way, they brought my boxes yesterday and I spent the day unpacking. Is there a garbage service set up to take away the boxes?"

"Yes, they're due this week and usually pick up every two weeks. Fold the boxes flat and stack them up at the curb with your other bins."

"Goodness, you're leading two lives aren't you Megg; secretary by day and secret operative the rest of the time. I promise after the surprise is sprung we will allow you to lead a normal life again."

"Oh thank-you Sarah, now I really have to go." I laugh and get to my car.

When I pull up to Highbridge, Thomas is just walking back to the kitchen from the garage. He stops in surprise as I park and walk toward him. Using an old excuse, I say "Just had to run to the Chemist's; be down in a jiffy," and walk away before he has time to say anything.

"O...okay, no rush." He does look rather quizzically at me as I pass by to disappear inside.

«»

"Jamie, have you noticed anything strange with Megg?"

He turns from the stove, "Well I have noticed she's out a lot in the day, but it is the holidays and we have a lot on the slate."

"Dad?" I ask of him as he sits with his face in the morning paper.

"What? Oh sorry Thomas, I was concentrating on this article. What's that you say?"

"Well, I just asked Jamie if he's noticed anything unusual about Megg lately."

"Megg?" Stephen asks with an innocent expression; "I've had her help Emily in preparation for the Christmas Eve celebration, could that be what you've noticed, Thomas?"

"Yes, I guess...probably...of course," I say and feel better that no one else has noticed Megg out of sorts besides me. She now appears around the corner with her bag, ready to go.

"Well, we're off to York for presents everyone; see you later at dinner, Stephen, call us if you think of anything we've missed on the list." She's quickly out the door so I follow her.

« »

I give Thomas and Meggs a little leeway of fifteen minutes then casually call out "Jamie, I have a couple of things to take care of this morning as well. Be back by lunch."

"Yes sir, lunch at 1pm," Jamie answers.

I walk to the garage and my car for a drive to Sarah's cottage.

"Stephen. Oh it's so good to see you." She gives me a big hug. "How nice of you to stop by, I know how busy you must be. Come in."

I step inside and notice with satisfaction Meggs has done a splendid job with the cottage.

"This is quite nice. What do you think of it?" I ask Sarah.

"It's wonderful Stephen, Megg did so much to make it comfortable and homey; I can't thank you both enough. Come in and sit down."

We go over our efforts for the move and agree it's gone much smoother than either of us had a right to expect. "It's almost scary." Sarah remarks with a laugh.

"Well, here's the thing," I launch into this morning's events with Thomas.

"Thomas is beginning to notice how busy Megg has been of late and asked Jamie and me this morning if we noticed it too."

"Oh no, do you think he's on to us?" Sarah asks.

"No, I don't think he has any idea that you're here, but I do think his eyes are open more than usual, shall we say. When did you plan to let him in on the surprise?"

"I planned to come to the party on Christmas Eve as a surprise when this began, but I've had doubts since I arrived. No doubts about him," I add, seeing Stephen's surprise, "I want to see him, I just don't think it would be fair to make him deal with 'us' in front of everyone at the party."

"I think that may be a wise consideration, my dear. You should follow your heart in these matters Sarah and it sounds like yours is speaking to you now," I tell her.

"I'll figure something out before Mom and Dad arrive and that's a promise," She assures me.

"I have no doubt whatsoever that you will Sarah. Anyone who can change her whole life around within three months can set up a meeting with the man she loves."

I walk to the door, "Anything you need here?" I ask her.

"No, Megg arranged everything to a tee and I'm fine," she answers and gives me another hug.

"Then we'll see you when you bring your parents around next week," I tell her.

I return to Highbridge and am surprised when Sarah calls to discuss 'a little plan'.

I'm down the stairs to dinner pretty pleased with myself this evening. So far, I've managed to remain true to Sarah and to Thomas during the past few weeks of subterfuge. Tonight's dinner will prove to be either a gigantic muck up or quite possibly the best work I've done so far I smile to myself.

"Good evening everyone." I enter the kitchen, rubbing my hands together and ask "Jamie, what's for dinner, I'm starving."

"Roast lamb, braised potatoes and green beans, sir."

"Splendid. And how are you son?"

"Fine Dad, you're in a good mood tonight, any particular reason?"

"Well son, I do have a reason. I've bought a cottage outside the Village for investment purposes."

He looks at me in astonishment and asks, "For investment purposes?"

"Yes, you know, lease it out; use it in summer for tourists, that sort of thing."

Thomas still looks stunned. I don't ordinarily do things spur of the moment or unplanned as a habit. I keep a straight face as he asks, "How long did it take to close this deal?"

"Oh about two weeks;" I answer, "got wind of a good deal and just decided to take advantage of it."

"Well then, I'm glad it went well. I just hope you find a renter soon to cover your expenses," Thomas says.

"Yes, well, there's the thing," I reply. "There is a current renter who refuses to leave and I hope you can go out there tomorrow and have a talk with him."

"Dad, if he doesn't move at your request, you may have to offer him some monetary persuasion," Thomas advises.

"That would be one way, but it doesn't look good does it for our family to buy someone out of their home. I mean, if we could do this with a heart to heart chat, wouldn't that be the better way?"

"Yes, I suppose it would Dad; I'll go tomorrow, where is this cottage?"

"It's down Long Street to the first lane on the right after the Village. There's just one cottage on the land so you can't miss it."

«»

This morning I dress in jeans and a sweater and walk to the kitchen to grab a quick bite before leaving.

"Good morning sir!" Jamie calls, "What can I get for you?"

"Morning Jamie. Just some toast and coffee for me, I have an errand to run for Dad."

With coffee, a piece of cinnamon toast and a quick look at the newspaper's front page, I'm off. An unpleasant task at best I think to myself, let's just get it over with and get on with the day.

On the drive over, it bothers me that this isn't like Dad to jump into something and then not see it through. He has aged and this might signal he's retired at the right time.

I find the first lane on the right and see the cottage further down the way. Parking in front, I take a deep breath for the unpleasant task and knock rather loudly on the door to show I expect a response. After a brief wait, I hear footsteps.

The door opens and I'm looking not at a man as expected, but into blue eyes framed by auburn hair and the most wonderful pair of lips I've ever known.

"Sarah. What....how did you get here...?"

Before I can say another syllable, my arms are full of her, for she's flung herself into them and is firmly lodged against me. It's amazing, unexpected, wonderful...she's really here, soft and warm in my arms.

We take time to look at each other and I tell her, "I don't care how this happened, just promise to stay here in my arms, please?"

"I will if you come inside because I am freezing," she laughs and shivering, she pulls me inside and helps take off my coat. I pull her directly back into my arms and we kiss long and tenderly, hungry for each other's touch.

"I've missed you so much," She whispers.

"Oh Sarah, you don't know how..." I pause to search for the word.

"Miserable you've been?" She says.

"Yes, yes it's been terrible, I can't eat, I sleep terribly and I can't keep my mind on my work." I hold her slightly away so that I can look at her.

"I'm in love with you," I tell her.

"I know."

"I have been since the first time I laid eyes on you."

"Me-too," She says.

"Wait, you know? And you are too?"

"Yes"

"Why didn't you tell me before you left...anything to indicate the least little spark?" I implore.

"I couldn't, Thomas. Something in me refused to let you in. I had to go away to find out what I wanted. Can you make sense of what I'm saying and forgive me?"

I look at the woman in front of me, tuck a tendril of her hair behind her ear then touch her cheek and hold her close.

"I won't let you go ever again," I tell her.

"I'll take that as a 'yes' she whispers into my ear.

We sit later in the kitchen eating sticky buns with coffee.

"So you've sold your house in America, applied for a visa and bought this house? Sarah, you are an absolutely awesome woman."

"It wouldn't have been possible without your Dad's help, he was the amazing one. We must have spent fifty hours on the phone. He put me in touch with the Estate agent who found this house. His attorney helped me with the visa application; and he offered me a job as the family genealogy researcher with a legitimate salary so that I could apply for the work-related visa."

"Okay, let me ask; has Megg been involved in any way?" I ask her.

Sarah laughs, "Oh yes, she had furniture brought from your attic to this house and added all the little personal touches you see here. She stocked the kitchen, arranged for the gas turn-on and the rubbish pickup. She's been here daily to check on me since I'm without a car and she's been a jewel."

"I knew it; she's always leaving, but when I would ask, she has a good excuse. Wait, were she and Dad the only ones in on this?"

"Yes, the others know nothing about it. We had to do it this way Thomas," Sarah says.

"Why? If you'd told me you wanted to come back, I'd have been there to help you move and would have had this house ready for you."

"I needed to come to you on my own, so that you could see there are no more walls inside me against you Thom."

I think about what she's saying for a few seconds. "I will be forever amazed that you did all this for me, thank-you, my love." I reach for her hand and kiss her palm and have a great idea.

"Come to the house and see everyone Sarah. They'll be so pleased...come now. Emily and Bart are decorating the Christmas tree and we can help them."

"Oh what fun; let me get my coat." She pauses to give me another kiss before going upstairs.

I have another thought and call after her, "Pack a bag and come stay at the house for the holidays."

She walks back down the stairs to look at me.

"Thomas, we haven't talked about our plans for the next few months, but I think this is a good time."

We sit in the lounge and she tells me that this house is her new home and she wants to work for Dad, but also to build her own genealogy business out of the cottage.

"I need to start my new life here in the Village and take time to adjust to my new country and circumstances."

"But what about us?" I ask her. "I want us to be together Sarah."

"We will be together and see each other every day. We'll get to know one another well, not in just a five week rush. There'll be time to talk to each other, share our childhood secrets, our teen years; what we want in the future, you with your mill, me with my business and we can help each other achieve our dreams." She lays her head on my shoulder.

"We can have many evenings together like this. And when the time is right, you can ask me to marry you."

"I have your permission do I?" I tell her. "Come here you; must you control all of my moves?" I kiss her until we're both breathless.

When I look, her face is shining, her eyes are closed. Just the way they should be I think with a smile. "Come on, let's go to Highbridge" and I pull her up from the couch.

« »

When we walk in the front door, Emily and Berty are already unpacking tree decorations in the great room. Thomas puts his finger to his lips so that I won't speak and we walk with quiet steps around the back of the room until we are behind them unnoticed.

"Merry Christmas." We call out in unison and startle Emily so much that she drops a box of ornaments, but Thomas catches it before they crash to the floor.

"Oh Mr. Thomas—Miss Sarah." She rushes over to give me a hug. "Are you here to help us celebrate? How long can you stay?"

"Forever," I answer, "I'm on a work visa."

"Oh how wonderful." She exclaims and Berty adds his congratulations as well. Then Emily addresses Thom.

"Mr. Thomas, you almost gave me a heart attack, those ornaments are older than you are."

"See how she treats me?" He lifts Emily off the floor to twirl her around a couple of times.

"Oh put me down Thom, put me down, or I swear I'll...." And he puts her down again.

"You're not too old for me to take a switch to and don't you forget it."

"Alright Ems, I'm sorry. Are you ok?"

"Yes, yes, now go on both of you and see the rest of the household." She calls after us as she puts her hair into place once more, "If you want to help in the decking of the halls, be back here in an hour."

Turning back to Berty rather out of breath after all the spinning around, she says in a low voice, "I think someone's in love; what do you think?" Berty nods his agreement and they get on with decorating plans for the tree.

Down in the kitchen we greet Jamie, who looks up in surprise, as pleased as Bert and Emily. "Welcome back Miss Sarah," he says to her.

"Where's Dad?" I ask.

"He's gone into York with Miss Margaret to shop sir. I believe he said he'd 'taken your place'?"

"Oh good lord, I was supposed to help Megg get presents for the rest of the children today. Was he upset?"

"No sir, not at all. In fact, he said 'On this occasion' he didn't mind at all filling in; said you'd know what he meant?" Jamie's voice ends on a high note.

"I believe he referred to the fact that he and Megg have been joined in secrecy against us all for weeks while they assisted Sarah in moving here from the States," I tell Jamie then say, "Isn't that right Sarah?"

She gives me a hug, "I confess to all and beg for mercy."

"Well and about time." Jamie comments as he looks at us with an all-knowing smile.

Chapter 9 Christmas Stars

My parents arrive on time at Manchester airport and both Thomas and I greet them at the terminal. It's been months since we've last seen each other and we hug until I remind them they need to pick up their baggage.

When I introduce Thomas, Dad shakes his hand with a firm grip and expresses pleasure at meeting him. Mom, of course, just gives him a big hug and says how happy she feels to 'meet the man of my daughter's affection'.

They both comment on my general glow of happiness, unstraightened hair and my sudden move from the U.S., but I feel their love and approval mixed with their surprise and that means a lot.

Thom and I lead them in their rental car through York and on to the Village. After parking behind my cottage, Pat jumps out to open Gloria's door and pauses to take in the hills in the distance.

Mom exclaims "Sarah, the house is adorable; we're so proud of you."

The men carry in the bags and place them upstairs in the guest room.

"This house is deceiving from the outside; it's pretty roomy in here," Pat observes, "even a guest bath, wow."

"Yes, the Estate agent said it used to be a vacation rental but that plan derailed when the previous owner passed unexpectedly." Thomas says. "Anyway, Sarah secured it and here we are."

Downstairs, Mom and I sit in the lounge and I light the fireplace. Thomas and Pat come down to join us and we talk and share time with Thomas as a part of our circle. This is wonderful, I think as I watch them together. They all seem at ease with each other.

"Well, I really must get back to see how Dad is managing," Thomas rises. "Pat and Gloria, it's good to meet you. Please come to the house whenever you like, Sarah can show you around, no need to stand on ceremony."

I follow Thom out to the car and give him a goodbye kiss.

"Thank-you Thomas for making them feel welcome."

"It was easy, they made it easy. See you soon love." He kisses me warmly again. "Bye." I watch him drive away and return to the cottage.

"Well," Mom says, "he is so nice and so handsome, too."

"What are his intentions?" Dad asks as Mom starts to sputter at him.

"Well Dad, that didn't take long," I say but smile at him.

"So? Dads want to know this stuff," He exclaims. "What does he do now that he's quit the family business? Does he have an income?"

"Yes Dad, he has an income. I think it will all become clear when we go to visit the Estate tomorrow. I'll give you a tour; we'll stop by the construction office to see the new mill they're building on Copper Swift; that's the stream running through Stephen's property. You'll be impressed, I promise." Then I think, heck, you're going to be blown away.

"Okay, what would you like to do now, you two?" I ask. "If you'd like a nap, please feel free to take one. If you're hungry, let's go to the kitchen. Just make yourselves comfortable, my home is yours."

I made breakfast for us early this morning and we've just piled into the car for a tour of the Village. Mom saw some shops yesterday on the way home she wants to check out, including Ted's Antiques.

When we stop in, we find Ted at the counter taking care of another customer. He waves and finishes up at the register before greeting us.

"Sarah, I didn't know you were back. When did you get in?" He gives me a friendly hug.

"Just a few days ago; I've applied for a work visa and live not far from here."

"Wow, you don't waste any time do you, that's great. What brought this on?"

"Let's just say Thomas has played a large part in my change of residence."

"Ah yes, I could see a spark there; couldn't happen to a nicer pair and I'm happy for you both."

"Thank you. Ted, I'd like you to meet my parents Pat and Gloria Sandlin of St Thomas. They're here for a holiday visit to check on their little girl."

He shakes hands with each of them. "You needn't worry about this one. She has singlehandedly unearthed more of the Smith's history in a few short months than anyone has done in a century." He turns back to me.

"Listen Sarah, I almost called Thomas, but since you're here, perhaps you'd like to hear more on the New Zealand Cross?"

"I would love to hear more, since I am now the official genealogist researcher for the family Smith."

"That's great news, congratulations." He goes to the counter and pulls a paper from underneath it.

"I kept this handy in case Thomas or Stephen came by; it's a list of those who were awarded the medal. It was first bestowed by the Queen earlier in New Zealand's history, however the time period that best fits your needs is early to mid-1860's, correct?'

"Yes, that's right," I answer him.

"Those medals were awarded by the Governor of New Zealand as their highest award. Long story short, though some felt this usurped the Queen's power, Victoria later ratified the governor's actions. As you can see, they were awarded for service during New Zealand's land wars to those who aided the Crown's forces. Look halfway down the list and tell me what you see," Ted directs.

I take a moment to read the names until I arrive at the one that means the most to me.

"Oh Ted, this is such good news. You didn't know this, but Thomas and I went to Aberdeen before I left and were able to get a partial translation of the sales agreement we found at the house. This is the first name of a man who signed it." I point to the name Daniel Smith.

"What can I say? It's another "ah-ha" moment for your work, congratulations, Sarah," He says.

"Not so fast, we still don't know his relationship until we find a link with Stephen's father, but it's exciting to know we may just find one as we progress. Thanks so much for your help, Ted."

Mom has been looking around the shop while we talk and comes to ask Ted about an antique clock. Dad sees how taken by it she is and decides to buy it as an early gift for Christmas. She's thrilled, refuses to have it shipped and carries it out of the shop with her.

I tactfully suggest, "I can ship that to you after the holidays if you want to leave it here."

"Oh no, this goes on the plane with me all the way, even if I have to ship my luggage. I don't trust anyone to take care of this," Mom says and Dad rolls his eyes.

"Okay Mom, but if you change your mind, let me know," I tell her. "How about we take a trip to Highbridge now and see what Thomas and his father have been working on?"

"Sounds good to me." Dad says, "Are you sure we should just walk in?"

"They're a very hospitable family, you'll see."

We drive through the Village and out the exact route that Thomas took when I first arrived. The gateposts soon come into sight, impressive with their wrought ironwork on top of two large granite columns. Dad throws a glance at Mom in the back seat as he turns in.

When we come over the rise and catch the first glimpse of the silvery granite house in the sun, I know their surprise; it's never failed to thrill me, no matter how many times I see it.

"Wow," Dad says, "I had no idea. That's quite a house; how old is it?"

"It was built over a hundred and twenty-five years ago. We believe Thomas' great grandfather assisted his grandfather with the plans," I tell him.

"It's beautiful." Mom has fallen under its spell, unable to take her eyes off it.

I guide Dad to a spot just past the front entrance to park the car. We climb the stairs to the terrace and I have them turn around to look out over the hill and down to the Copper Swift's path through the fields and woods of the valley. The first storey of granite has been laid on the foundation before the holiday shut-down and I can't wait to go see it with Thomas.

"Let's go in and see the house then we can visit the Mill afterward," I tell them.

Berty opens the door and greets me warmly; "Miss Sarah, please come in."

"Berty, I'd like you to meet my parents Pat and Gloria Sandlin from St. Thomas. This is Berty," I tell my parents, "one of the prime members of Highbridge's staff. He takes good care of the house and assists Emily, the chief housekeeper.

"Thomas knew we'd be up today and said to show Mom and Dad around the house. Is Stephen in today?"

"No, Miss Sarah; he's gone off on some errands for the celebration. May I assist you?"

"No, we'll be fine Berty, thank-you. Could you tell Emily we're here and perhaps she could break and come by to meet my parents?"

"Of course, Miss Sarah." Berty walks down the hall and leaves us to wander as desired.

I decide to take them upstairs first to see my room. Just as I left it I think as we step inside; the bed is made up and fresh towels are in the bathroom.

"How pretty this is." Mom exclaims, "You must have been so pleased when you came here."

"Yes, I was very surprised by it all and had no idea what I'd experience. That view as you came up the driveway was my first clue; not your quaint little English cottage, right?" I laugh and they nod in agreement.

"A nice surprise though, right?" Dad asks.

"It's wonderful and so much fun, every day a different discovery. But the best part is the people; Thom and his father and the staff members who keep it running so smoothly. I want you to meet them all and see what I mean. Let's go downstairs and I'll show you where we congregate the most." My parents smile at each other as they walk with me and seem impressed with the house.

I show them the great room and Mom, the antique lover, is amazed by its size.

"I love the fireplaces and those French doors down the side. Oh, what beautiful old furniture and lamps, this room is wonderful." She exclaims and we continue to cross to the dining room.

They're impressed with the size of the banquet-sized table and beautiful chandeliers. The portraits draw Dad's attention while Mom wanders around the edges of the room to admire the crystal.

"You should see it at night, but you'll get a chance on Christmas Eve," I add.

Dad is rather quiet and stands looking through one of the large French doors out to the terrace and gardens.

"Penny for your thoughts, Dad," I say as I walk up behind him.

"I'm thinking this is more than I could ever have provided you my daughter and yet if I could, I would have."

"I know that Dad, but... my little cottage that I love so much...you and Mom provided that with the money you gave me for college."

"Really? Good for you Sarah. You've a base of your own to build on; I was concerned you were dependent on someone else to provide your quality of life, but it's good to hear you've taken charge. I feel much better." He gives me a hug.

"Keep a small part of yourself independent Sarah," Dad adds, "it's the best advice I can give you. That way if something fails or goes awry, you have a fall back plan. I know you'll always be with Thomas, but life can throw some pretty mean punches and its best to give yourself every option you can."

"Thanks Dad, I do understand your intention and appreciate your concern, but you see I've known those things since Brian left." I give him a kiss on the cheek then turn so Mom can hear me from the other side of the room.

"Come on you two, it's lunch time in the kitchen." I lead them down the back stairs and into the kitchen where Stephen, Megg and Emily are already seated. Jamie is just dishing up something delicious from a pot on the stove.

"Have room for three more?" I ask. Stephen jumps up in surprise and comes to greet my parents.

"Wonderful to see you both; good flight in and all?" He asks them.

"Yes, no problems, smooth flight all the way," Dad answers and I introduce them to each of my friends.

Stephen invites Mom to the table; "Please, have a seat Gloria." He pulls out a chair for her by Megg.

"Pat, come over here by me," he directs next; "I think we have something in common."

"Oh boy," Thomas says as he enters, "watch out when he says that; he usually has ulterior motives." He gives me a peck on the cheek then one for my Mom as well, who turns a nice shade of consequent pink.

"Well now, wait a minute..." Stephen says over the laughter.

"I've been very busy in my search for a Father Christmas and haven't found one. Then Sarah happened to mention that you, Pat," he turns toward him, "played a very good Santa for years at the school where you taught. Is that true?" He asks with an innocent look.

Dad glances at me as I try to hold back a smile and stare at him with my largest deer–in–the–headlights look.

"Since my daughter has spilled the beans, yes that's true, but it's been several years and I'm pretty rusty."

"Oh Pat, I'm afraid we are unable to accept that as a plausible excuse," Stephen appears very serious, "but I'm sure you didn't mean it that way. Would you please be our Father Christmas this year?"

Mom gives him a "go ahead dear" look, but Dad has already decided.

"Stephen, I'd be honored." He breaks into a smile and they shake hands on it.

From then on, lunch becomes a "get acquainted party" over some of Jamie's delicious vegetable soup and homemade bread. At one point, Gloria even joins Jamie at the kitchen counter to trade traditional holiday recipes.

Afterwards, while Thomas takes Pat down to the construction site, Mom goes with Megg to see plans for the rest of the decorations, leaving me some time with Stephen.

"Well my dear, it's all gone quite nicely so far, don't you think?" He says and sips from a second cup of coffee.

"Yes it's more than I could have hoped for; in fact I think this may be the best Christmas ever. Thank-you for

Dad's part in your plans by the way, I think he was quite flattered to be asked."

"You are welcome and he is the logical choice; experience and excellent references. Besides I'm sure he feels like a duck out of water with all of us relative strangers in this old house. I want both your parents to feel at ease with us for the holidays."

"I think you've hit on the very thing that will do just that."

"Sarah, I want a word with you in confidence, if you don't mind?" He seems serious.

"Of course, is anything wrong?"

"No, in fact, I've decided to ask Megg to marry me."

"Oh Stephen, that's just wonderful." I come around the table and hug his neck.

"You think it's a good idea then, not silly at my age?"

"I think it's a terrific idea and what age do you mean? You have so much energy and spirit; I know you two have many good years ahead of you."

"Good, I value your opinion and though I've already consulted Thomas, I wanted to hear from you too."

"I think you should ask her as soon as possible. Choose a place away from everyone and pull out a ring Stephen, it's the best way to do it."

"Good advice dear and I've already purchased a ring for the occasion, would you like to see it?" He looks around to make sure we are alone then pulls a box out of his jacket pocket and opens the lid to show me the diamond ring inside.

"Beautiful. Good choice, she'll love it, now put it away before the surprise gets ruined." He stuffs the box back in his pocket just as Thomas and Pat return.

"Well, what do you think of our new Mill so far, Pat?"

"It's going to be state of the art, no doubt about it. I told Thomas that an uncle of mine in Connecticut had a mill on his property, built by his grandfather long before aluminum paddle wheels and pressure treated wood. By the time I reached high school it was almost gone. With the granite and that new wheel of yours, this Mill will be around for generations. I'd like to come back and see it when it's in operation."

"I think you'll be back here many times." Stephen said and winked at Pat, who got it and winked back.

《》

Mom and Dad decided to return to the cottage and relax a little; I believe the plan was 'to sit around in our pj's and watch the fire'. I've remained here to spend time with Thomas. In the library, we catch up on the day with each other and Ted's news is first.

"That's amazing. Have you told Dad yet?" Thom asks.

"No, I haven't, it's sort of been lost in all the holiday preparations; I think it can wait a little, don't you?"

"Yes, I suppose it can, in consideration of the other news. Did Dad tell you about Megg?"

"He did. Isn't it wonderful? I think they make a grand match. They've had enough years to know each other so well."

"I told him the same, speaking of which, come here you, let's continue this 'get to know each other better' stuff, shall we?" He wraps me in a hug and kisses me soundly.

"I could get used to this." I inform him.

« »

Christmas Eve dawns a little cloudy, with even a chance of some snow predicted for northern areas near Scotland's borders. I believe we are well ready for tonight's celebration but I continue to do a final inspection. To say I've been busy would be a total understatement as the name "Emily!" has been called out several times today to summon my help for one thing or another.

Jamie's been baking daily for the holidays and with each new batch he pulls from the oven, the tantalizing aroma drifts upstairs through the house. It soon draws marauders down to the kitchen for tastes and any available crumbs about, until he chases all away and out from under foot. His tasty creations are set out every evening for milk and cookie seekers and by morning he notes with satisfaction not a cookie survives.

John's two assistants from the Village forage enough greenery from the Estate woods to decorate inside the

276

house, as well as over the main gates and the front entrance. To top it off, Stephen directs them to drape fairy lights around the door and out the terrace rails.

Inside, Megg, Berty and Stephen, with help from Pat and Gloria, rally to help put up bay leaves from the herb garden combined with holly and cedar boughs; they apply them to the stair rails, around both fireplaces and on the rails above the great room. In a few short hours, the fragrance fills the large room and hallway.

I have several branches brought to the dining room where I add them to the tables and finish with sparkly tinsel, fairy lights and candles then stand back to admire my handiwork.

"I say, good job Ems, really first-class." Mr. Stephen says from the doorway.

"It's been a labor of love and such a joy to see all this come back to us, as it used to be," I tell him.

"Yes, I feel the same," He answers. "Now go enjoy some time for yourself. Big night and you've done more than enough to prepare; you deserve some time of your own."

"Thank you Sir, I will; that is if you have no loose ends to be dealt with?"

"No Emily, everything is perfect, now go."

With a last check on the large tree in the great room as I as pass through, I see the lights and higher decorations are all in place with additional decorations laid out properly for the guests who wish to help finish the lower limbs tonight.

This year's tree reflects the new hope and expectations of our Highbridge family I think and say a little prayer of thanks for all that has occurred this year.

I go over details for the evening as I climb the stairs. Donald and Dee Ferguson arrived earlier with their two teenagers and are in their rooms for a little rest after their long road trip; the other guests from the Village will start arriving around six, which leaves me just enough time to prepare myself for the night's festivities.

« »

I've lit the tree lights and stand by the fireplace, relishing the warmth, staring into its flames, as I imagine many of my forbearer's did. How grateful I feel that Sarah has come to help us know some of them.

Footsteps in the upstairs hallway prompt me to turn; Meg watches me as she comes down the stairs. She's wearing blue velvet with some sort of sparkly shawl around her shoulders; quite a wonderful sight I think.

"Good evening Megg." I take her hand, "How beautiful you look my dear, come sit with me by the fire. That dress looks wonderful on you."

"Why thank you Stephen. Sarah and I went shopping last week. Oh my, and doesn't the tree look pretty with all its lights," Margaret exclaims.

"Yes, rather majestic in that corner of the room," I agree with her. "Berty dared to lean over the second floor rail to place the silver star." I lead her to two chairs I've placed in front of the tree and we sit down together.

"I enjoyed shopping with you yesterday."

"Such fun wasn't it?" She smiles at me, "It's been a long time since I felt that carefree."

"For me too, Megg."

"Ah, but you have so much family around you Stephen; surely you must feel so appreciated," She remarks.

"Yes of course, but I have no one to really enjoy simple things like shopping or just sitting in front of the fire as we are right now. I've thought about that a lot, seeing Thomas and Sarah so happy together. It's reminded me how much nicer it is when one has someone special who cares."

I take her hand and hold it, which seems to surprise her.

"Margaret, we've spent a lot of years together."

"Haven't we though," she answers, "more than some married couples." I smile at her reply and wait for an opening to say more. Meg seems to sense it and remains quiet, her hand still in mine.

"I have a special spot in my heart for you Megg, have had for some time. Do you think you could grow to appreciate me as well?" I ask her.

"Stephen, I hold you in the highest regard and truthfully, you already hold a place in my heart as well." I look down at her hand in mine, return to look into her eyes, then reach into my pocket and withdraw the ring case. She draws up her breath in surprise as I show her the diamond ring inside.

"My dear Megg, would you please consent to be my wife and allow me to honor you and take care of you the way you've taken care of me all these years?"

She remains quietly looking into my eyes and seems to see my deepest feelings there. For just a moment I imagine she has thoughts of her late husband even as I remember my dear Irene. But Megg suddenly has a look of clarity in her expression and she answers my question clearly.

"I realise I want to spend the rest of my life with you, yes Stephen, I will."

I place the ring on her finger and pull her from the chair and into my arms. Our kiss seals the promise and just at that moment the doorbell rings as guests begin arriving. I loosen my arms to look at her.

"My timing may be a little off," I say in humility.

She smiles at me, "There's nothing wrong with your timing dear, it's the rest of the world that's a little off." We laugh and walk together to greet the guests.

Emily and Bert are kept very busy leading guests into the great room and are pleased to see their reaction to the tree; especially the children who are excited by its lights and sheer size. Games have been set up in the other end of the room and soon the Ferguson teens join in to help with the ten little guests who share all sorts of Christmas fun.

<< >>

Thomas greets my parents and me at the front door with a "Hello, Merry Christmas" then kisses mom and me before addressing Dad.

"Merry Christmas, Pat" he offers his hand, but Dad grabs him in a rough hug with a thump on the back. "Right back at you! Great decorations by the way," Dad says in appreciation, "we could see them from down the road."

"Thank you; tell that to Stephen, he'll be so proud. Come in, come in, Dad and Megg are in the great room."

"I understand there will be an announcement later tonight." Thomas whispers to me as we walk down the hall then returns to his role as host.

"What can I get you to drink, Pat? We have some fruit punch over here on the table, as well as wine and should you want, I have some very good sherry."

"Thank you Thomas, but since Father Christmas may visit tonight, I believe abstinence would be the way to go. I'll just settle for some sparkling seltzer with a twist."

Thomas turns to me to whisper, "You look very beautiful tonight my darling."

"Thank-you sir and so do you. I think this is the first time I've seen you in a tuxedo."

"Well, my dearest girl came so I wanted to put on my best." He bends to kiss my cheek.

Guests are invited to place ornaments on the tree and children join in to adorn the lower branches. Time passes as neighbors greet one another and share their good wishes. Occasional laughter breaks out over a joke well-told, or something that happened during the past year.

Dinner is announced and as I wait to enter the dining room with Thomas, I hear "oohs" and "ahhs" from the other guests ahead of us. When we enter, I understand why.

The lights in the chandeliers have been dimmed to set the mood and the table sparkles with its own fairy lights. Candles in high-pedestal, cut-glass candle stands are reflected by tinsel tucked into greenery down the full length of the table. Stephen has chosen some lively string music to be played during dinner and the greenery scents of Christmas permeate the room with their woodsy fragrance, making it a treat for all our senses.

Emily earlier bedecked the children's special table with sparkling lights, teddy bears and other toys and the children are eager to find their seats and claim their crackers at each setting. She and John sit with them at the far end of the dining room, close enough to see parents but enough away that a little noise won't bother the other guests.

When everyone finds their seat, Stephen takes his place at the head of the table and taps his glass; guests settle down to give him their full attention.

"I want to thank all of you for sharing your Christmas Eve with us at Highbridge. Many years ago tradition brought our friends from the Village to help us celebrate and with this event, we're extremely happy to reestablish the tradition." Someone starts to applaud and all join in as Stephen acknowledges proudly.

"We've been very blessed to return to this house on a fulltime basis from the London business world. As you may have noticed, there is a new endeavor underway here; the Copper Swift Mill for artisan stone-milled flours will be completed this summer and we hope to offer some employment opportunities." Again applause, as it is welcome news.

"We have wonderful new friends of my son's with us tonight; Miss Sarah Sandlin and her family, Pat and Gloria of St Thomas. Sarah visited last October and liked it so much, she applied for a visa and bought a house in the Village. Welcome to you all."

"I also wish to announce that tonight," he pauses and turns to Megg on his right, "this lovely lady, Miss Margaret Jenkins, formerly of London, was asked to be my wife and she has accepted." Applause breaks out in earnest then and Stephen reaches over to take Megg's hand for a kiss.

"And let us not forget what it is we celebrate tonight; the birth of a tiny baby born far from here, into poverty, sent by God to save us all. Let us honor Him in this house tonight and always.

"So please lift your glasses to each other and wish us all a very Merry Christmas and the happiest of New Years." He touches his glass first with Margaret's as the sound of ringing crystal spreads down the table. The children are told to pop their crackers at that very moment, their laughter comes loud and clear as confetti flies and they open their party hats to put upon their heads.

Dinner is served by Berty, Jamie and John's two young charges from the village who agreed to train as servers for the occasion. The first course, lobster bisque, creamy in its richness, is served with a white chardonnay. Next come plates of thinly sliced roast beef with a red-wine gravy and sides of little potatoes, glazed carrots and a ratatouille. Jamie's small loaves of bread and creamery buttery in little pots are set between guests to share.

Conversations quiet a little as everyone savors and consumes the delicious meal; candles burn low as we finally sit back to enjoy each other's company. Little ones begin to squirm at the children's table and all agree they can't eat another morsel.

"Dessert will be available in the great room, so please everyone come join us there," Stephen announces, "so that we can recover a little." He and Meg begin to leave the table amid laughter at his remark and lead the way. Parents and children are guided to seats in front of the tree and the remainder of guests choose comfortable seating for themselves.

A sudden sound of sleigh bells can be heard somewhere above them and the children fall silent as they turn toward the upstairs rail. There appears Father Christmas and he laughs "Ho-Ho-Ho" as he waves to them. They cheer and call out his name; he begins to throw candies down to them from his pockets, creating quite a hubbub until they've scrambled to retrieve every piece.

Then Father comes down the staircase with his huge bag dragging behind him and makes his way to the tree, the children moving with him. He's resplendent in red with white fur trim, a sprig of holly is tucked into his cap and his belly makes him appear very well fed.

"Brrr, it's cold flying outside tonight children and I must hurry to take presents to boys and girls all over the world." he declares. "But first I thought you might like a present right now before you go home, would you like that?"

A resounding cheer goes up from the children and he calms them by saying "Good. Now, everyone find Mom and Dad and we'll start. This little girl right over here will be first to come up and when she returns to her seat, the next child in the row may come up and so forth; everyone understand? Mom and Dad you may have to assist," he winks at the parents.

I've seen Dad do this so many times that it brings a tear to my eye and Thomas puts his arm around my shoulders to give me a squeeze as we watch the scene unfold. The huge bag of toys is emptied one by one until children from the smallest to the oldest receive a gift.

"Now boys and girls, I have to hurry away, but if you're all very good in the coming year, I'll see you again. He turns and ascends the stairs, pausing at the top to call "Merry Christmas!" With a wave of his arm over his head, he disappears into the upstairs hallway where shortly we hear sleigh bells begin and fade away.

Everyone including the adults, cheers and claps at the wonderful 'visit' then desserts are served from the tables along the side of the room with fresh coffee and beverages for the children as well.

Pat rejoins us and laughter fills the room until the hour grows late and guests start to leave with their sleepy children. Small boxes of Jamie's cookies, shortbreads, chocolates and the like, are handed to the guests at the door as Stephen with Megg at his side and Thomas and I wish them a very Merry Christmas.

Later we all sit in the great room talking about our favorite parts of the evening. Thomas has poured scotch for the men; the ladies sip Irish coffee.

"Pat, you exceeded expectations and revived even my belief in Father Christmas tonight." Stephen declares.

"You should have seen the children's eyes when you jingled those bells upstairs," Megg comments, "they were as wide as saucers."

"And the candy over the rail was genius," Thomas adds.

Pat starts to get a little embarrassed at all the praise, "Thank you everyone, I had a great time and it was so much fun for me too. I've never played Father Christmas before and now I can add that to my 'resume'."

Stephen pigeonholes him with "Well, you'll be returning for many years after that performance."

Thomas and I leave the group soon after Stephen's banter with Dad. We put on coats with scarves to walk outside across the terraces into the chilly evening. The greenery and fairy lights along the rails are beautiful and I put my hand in Thomas' warm jacket pocket where he covers it with his. The silence of the countryside settles upon us.

"You can imagine Christmas peace all over the world can't you?" I whisper as I gaze at the lights along the way.

"It is serene out here after the din of the party." Thomas replies.

The windows of the house are lit and golden in the night; the smells of cedar boughs along the terrace mixed with fireplace smoke hang in the crisp air. Somewhere across the fields a hound bays at some unfortunate hare or fox.

"This is my first Christmas in the U.K. It's been special for so many reasons, but mainly because you're here Thom."

« »

I stop walking and turn to pull Sarah closer, I see her face lit by the soft light of the decorations and kiss her with all the passion I feel for her.

Letting her go a little, I reach into my overcoat pocket and bring out something I've been waiting to give her in a special time.

"I have a present for you." I take her left hand and slip the beautiful ring on her finger. Its stone flashes as she looks down at it, the lights of Christmas catch perfectly in its center and reflect back to her gaze.

"It's my mother's ring." I pause at her memory, "A perfect blue diamond with white diamonds around it, what she used to call her 'stars' and I want you to have it." With my hand under her chin, I gently bring her eyes to mine.

"You are the stars in my life Sarah. Promise that you'll marry me...sometime in the near future? I vow to you, there is no other woman for me."

She wraps her arms around my neck, burying her face for a moment then lifts her eyes to mine.

"Yes Thomas, I vow this night to be only yours." She seals the promise with the warmth of her lips on mine.

We stay together for a while on the terrace, warm in our embrace, looking up at the night sky and all its stars laid out above us. We listen to its peace and seal it into our memories for all the years to come.

« »

Chapter 10 Ahnentafel

Boxing Day dawns bright and beautiful for a most welcome and more casual celebration from yesterday's.

The kitchen table is almost filled to capacity for the first time since I came to Highbridge; Donnie, Dee and their teens have stayed; Stephen and Margaret sit next to each other; Bert and Emily and even John and his two gardeners from the Village; Joseph and Dorothy McHugh; my Thomas; mom and dad. Of course Jamie joins us as soon as the food is on the table.

"I'd like to share something with everyone." Thomas stands to speak and we all quiet down.

"Last night on Christmas Eve I asked Sarah to marry me, at some point in the not too distant future and she said 'Yes'." He finishes proudly and breaks out a big smile.

Everyone laughs and applauds, some get up to embrace and congratulate us. Mom sheds tears and Dad puts his arm around her until she regains control. Stephen shakes Thomas's hand saying "Congratulations boy. Well done."

Stephen comes to me now and gives me a bear hug, saying in my ear for no one else's benefit, "Welcome to our family my dear daughter," which instantly touches my heart that he should think of me in that way.

Everyone sits back down to attack the food on the table with gusto. I take the opportunity to get acquainted with Donnie and Dee's two teens; Duncan at seventeen who wants to be a doctor and is a senior this year; his sister Aileen, sixteen and going on twenty as Dee lovingly describes her, has no aspirations as yet but does love to play her guitar.

In the afternoon the men 'chill out' from the previous days' formality and watch football while snacking at will. We girls observe another tradition and go to the Village to shop sales all afternoon. The evening finds us together again at a supper buffet; traditional ham, scrumptious leftovers and of course, a Christmas cake to be dealt with.

Sure enough, as I weigh myself this morning, I discover an extra five pounds since last week's weigh-in. I make an early New Year's vow into the bathroom mirror; "No more sweets and half your plate will be vegetable."

The past few days hover in the back of my mind, so magical with Thomas's proposal, Stephen and Megg's engagement and sharing my new family with Mom and Dad.

We all stayed at Highbridge last night and they've decided to skip breakfast to get an early start for the Manchester airport.

"Bound to be busy with all the holiday travelers and we don't want to miss our flight," Dad says as we walk with them out to the driveway.

"We love you," Mom hugs me, tears welling up in her eyes.

"Now don't start or I'll be right there with you," I tell her.

Dad intervenes; "Ok you two, what happened to that Brit stuff; stiff upper lip and all?" We both start to laugh and reach for tissue.

He hugs me; "Now listen—keep in touch. We want to hear more on your research into Thomas' family. Sounds like you've found some intriguing stuff."

"And call me if you reach an agreement on wedding plans," Mom instructs, "I don't want to find out two weeks beforehand."

"Yes Mom, I will." They're both into the car and off down the drive with waves and more tears, I suspect.

Don wants to meet with Thomas and me before he leaves. Stephen and Meggs have gone off to York and we'll catch them up later with Don's findings on the documents.

We meet in the library and he takes charge; "Let me walk you through this first then if you have questions, which I'm sure you will, you can ask them when I've finished."

"I received an answer from the Archives via an old friend who let us say, 'accelerated the process' a little?" He smiles as we sit down at the library table.

"Donnie," I interject quickly, "I hope you don't mind, but I've brought a tape recorder so we don't lose any of our discussion this morning. It isn't often that I get the professional input of someone with your knowledge and expertise."

"Well Sarah, on behalf of all battered university professors everywhere, I thank you," he quips, "and the recorder is a good idea, but I've brought you each a packet with a summary of findings, as well."

"The land coordinates in both the documents match a well-known Aberdeenshire granite quarry which was active from the mid-19th century and closed in 1966. Two men on the partnership papers founded the quarry and a third, your boy Angus, was added as partner within a few years. You'll see I've had the document transcribed into English for you with visible names and the terms of the agreement."

Thomas notes with surprise as he reads the summary, "One of the original partners is a Daniel Smith."

"This may be our answer to how Angus gained ownership of the land between 1873 and 1886 when he sold it; Daniel could be his father," I theorize.

"Or an uncle, perhaps even a cousin; it's a lead which you'll get use from I'm sure," Don remarks then continues.

"Alright, a summary of the last document is on page three in your packets. This is the oldest of the documents and dated April of 1868. I find it of most interest because the language is a mix of English, Gaelic and German; it contains the seal of the Queen's Representative in Dunedin, New Zealand."

"You're saying this document originated in New Zealand?" Thomas asks.

"That's affirmative; the seller sold some farm property to two buyers, both with the last name of Shepherd. Unfortunately the ink on this one hundred forty year old document has been irreparably damaged and much of the contract's detail is obscured, including first names of the buyers and the complete name of the seller.

"But here's an interesting fact," Don adds, "I obtained a lab exam of the document and though it didn't help with the writing itself, it did show residual salt on the paper, a curious discovery. It indicates to me the damage to the inked document is probably not all from the U.K.'s insidious moisture but perhaps from a much earlier exposure to sea water."

"Such as a voyage back to the U.K.?" I ask.

"That possibility comes to mind Sarah, the seller remains a mystery at this point, but I'm sure you know from experience, there's more than one way to approach the barn so-to-speak; you may prefer to come from another angle. Since the document bears the seal of the Queen's Rep. there may be record of the transaction on the books in Dunedin or at Wellington, the Capital at that time."

"You're right Donnie," I agree with him, "there's a definite New Zealand connection we're onto between your findings and the medals."

"New Zealand is certainly not my forte, Sarah, so I did what any red-blooded, new millennium professor would do and queried New Zealand's history online; there's a fact sheet in your packets.

"In review I found several possibilities for your Mr. Smith's presence in N.Z. The English and Dutch along with other nationalities were early on the island from around 1792 to 1800 as sealers and whalers. The Maori called them Pakehas or 'white people'.

"Then there were settlers who took the land they wanted and were subject to native tribesmen taking what they felt was theirs in exchange. Mariners who wished to leave their ships and conduct trade with the natives sometimes negotiated to obtain a "title" to pieces of land from Maori chieftains. Some wound up as slaves used as translators for the tribe with English-speaking Europeans.

"Your Mr. Smith could also have been a member of the British East India Trading Company who added New

Zealand to their trade route in 1779." Don takes a sip of his coffee before continuing.

"There were land wars among the tribes themselves from 1845 through 1872 and at that time the British Monarchy appointed Sir George Grey as Governor and stationed British soldiers to protect settlers and beat back the natives. Some of the soldiers stayed to live after 1872 and their descendants live there today."

"So as I understand it," Thomas says, "our choices for Mr. Smith are: English ex-pat who jumped ship; whale hunter; seal hunter; member of the British East Trading Company; or a British soldier who stayed long enough to claim his own land."

"Those are the obvious choices, but don't forget that settlers were heading "down under" for some time while all of this went on." I remind them both.

"Sounds like a pretty massive research project to me Sarah, but you do have several leads as a result of these documents." He jokes, "Perhaps I'll check back with you in about thirty years."

"Now just a minute Donnie, Ted informs me the medals were also awarded to volunteer colonists aiding the British during the land wars, so that may help us narrow down the actual window of time."

"You're right; good thought and I know you'll keep after that clue. But to get back to the root of the matter;

did the Mr. Smith in question accumulate enough wealth to invest in Aberdeen land in 1873 as a silent partner?"

"And second," Thomas adds, "what did he do to generate that wealth since he sold his property rather cheaply?"

"We can go back to the natural resources of the era" I offer, "Seal skins did reach a high trade value in that period as they were used for men's tall hats and women's coats."

"But it just isn't plausible that our man could raise the amount needed with hides." Thomas adds.

"Sorry Sarah,' Don says, "I have to agree with Thomas. But here's a thought; what about the New Zealand Company? They were founded in 1825 and though somewhat inadequate with their organization and practices, they did manage to stay afloat for a period to about 1852. In 1843, they established an office in Edinburgh to encourage people to emigrate from Scotland to a 200,000 acre town called New Edinburgh. The town my friends, became Dunedin in 1847 and was located on the central-east coast of Otago, the South Island of New Zealand."

"That would be a possible option if we can prove that Daniel or Angus Smith came from Scotland."

"It's a variable Sarah. The land sale document also indicates the property was crossed by a stream northwest of Dunedin," Don says.

"I'm not getting your point," Thomas remarks.

"Sorry, of course you're not because it reminds me of something I read," Donnie apologizes. "There was a gold discovery at a place called Gabriel's Gully in 1862." He stops and waits for Thomas and me to catch up with his implication.

"Oh my gosh," I exclaim, "the gold watch fob."

"What's the location of that Gully?" Thomas asks Don.

"Otago," Don replies, "northwest of Dunedin and off the Tuapeka River near Lawrence."

We all go silent as we wind through the chain of events in our minds and the gravity of the new theory takes hold.

"Okay you two," Thomas directs, "let's get a grip here; you theorize and that's all it is at this point, you do know that don't you?" Donnie and I both nod.

"Your theory is that for whatever reason, my alleged great, great grandfather lived in New Zealand and we know that because of the medal awarded him for service in the land wars. Correct so far?" We nod again.

"Second, the land agreement sold property located within some miles of an actual 1862 gold rush in the Otago area. He sold the property in 1868 and Mr. Smith had in theory at least six years to mine whatever gold he could find on his property or elsewhere, correct?" More nods.

Thomas pauses then asks, "What did gold sell for in that period of time?"

"Somewhere around three pounds per troy ounce or eighteen dollars American." Don answers then adds some clarity, "The real question here though, is how to link Daniel and Angus Smith with Charles Smith? Without that we're just shooting in the dark." With that question, he effectively slows the wild train we're all riding.

"I agree Donnie," I tell him. "When I did the suggested timeline it appears we're missing a generation in order for the dates on these documents to link with those of Thomas' grandfather Charles."

We end the discussion so that Donnie and his family can get on the road. It's been a fascinating morning and my head is swimming with the facts and theories on the table for Thomas' great, great grandfather. Now it's up to me to find the proof and to do that I'll continue to explore resources in Scotland as well as in New Zealand.

If I can find a list of registered miners in New Zealand...my stomach does a little jump, perhaps even make a trip to N.Z...the idea sounds thrilling.

"Safe trip to you all." I call to Donnie and his family as he loads up in the front driveway.

"Call me." Don says to us as he closes the car door.

"You're first on the list Don; thanks again." Thomas calls back then puts his arm around my shoulders as we return to the front door.

"This day has been amazing," Thom remarks, "too bad Dad isn't here; he'll be so excited when he hears Don's news."

"Absolutely, but he's with Margaret checking out honeymoon destinations at the travel office."

"Ah then it's good they're not here," Thom remarks.

"Why?" I ask as we walk up the front steps.

"I have a feeling Meggs wouldn't like to spend her honeymoon in the dusty record rooms of New Zealand," He replies.

"What would be wrong with that?" I ask, stealing a look at him to see his reaction.

He catches the impishness in my gaze and suddenly knows what I'm thinking; we'll have need of a honeymoon destination at some point.

"You! I'm onto your plan, always one step ahead aren't you." He kisses me playfully at first but it lengthens into something more.

"Well?" I ask when we finally come up for air.

"Maybe," He answers and though he tries to conceal the look in his eyes, it tells me he would do just about anything for me, the love of his life.

End

Epilogue

I enter the store early to take down decorations and put them away for the year. Dad decided this morning to take an extra day off at home and the thought of the Smiths' desk stored in the back room gave me extra motivation to come in. In fact, it's been 'calling' to me ever since we unloaded the truck and this will be a good time to take care of it while things are slow.

In the back room, I pull the huge desk on its dolly away from the wall and push it to a well-lit space. The dust cover comes off and the unusual look of the wood is again impressive. Covered by decades of dust and dirt, it'll involve some serious detailing with hand rubbing, but I can't think of a better job to follow the holidays.

I take a small stiff brush to the carvings on the front and side panels to remove embedded dirt then do an initial rubdown of all its surfaces with Tung oil on a soft cloth. The heavy buildup areas over the drawer pulls and on the top work surface need extra rubbing, but soon respond to the oil's magic as the grain of the wood begins to show through.

Three hours later and we're getting there I think as I prepare to do a final wipe-down to preserve its finish into the future. The wood is showing an inner pearly sheen as its hidden grain wakes up and starts to look fantastic, like day and night from the way it was in the attic. Sarah and Thomas will love it.

I replace the lid on the tung oil can, set it down on the corner of the desk and turn to the tool bench for a clean cloth. But I stop when I hear a soft "click" behind me and turn around to investigate. Now a faint sliding sound of wood on wood begins and I see a drawer emerge from the fretwork and carvings along the desk's edge, directly under the spot where the oil can sits.

"I'll be....vibration from the can must have set it loose," I say out loud in my surprise.

I peer inside the drawer and recognize the handle of an old pistol where some coarse red cloth has fallen away. The gun's barrel is darkened with age but it still reflects light from the overhead spotlight. A leather thong is wrapped around the gun's handle with a strange curved pendant about the size of a half dollar attached to it. There are carvings in it resembling Aboriginal work and it's a green stone, like jade. Then I remember Sarah's research; maybe New Zealand jade.

I shine my flashlight to the back of the drawer where a third object the size of my fist catches the light...I stare spellbound at its soft gold surface.

Arrival - April 18, 1848

I look skyward from my stance at the ship's rail. A flock of sea gulls circles and dives for food; stealing from vendors' baskets on the wharf, their shrill cacophony provides background to the noisy scene below me. The assaulting odor of fish mixed with the smell of the harbor makes me feel a sensory overload after three months on this tall ship.

DANIEL SMITH

New Zealand Passage

Book Two in the Trilogy of Thomas's family.

May 2015